# Montana Cowboy Promise

# MONTANA COWBOY PROMISE

## A Wyatt Brothers Romance

### JANE PORTER

TULE
PUBLISHING

# DEDICATION

*For the best little publishing team—*
*Meghan, Cyndi, Nikki, Lee, Sinclair, Julie & Kelly*
*Love working with all of you*
*You make Tule fun!*

# Chapter One

TOMMY WYATT TUGGED his cowboy hat a little lower keeping the light drizzle off his face. Rain was good for Central California as Monterey County grew important crops—strawberries, lettuce, tomatoes, spinach and more—but he wasn't sure if this was fog or rain. Either way, tonight's rodeo was held at an indoor arena, which would keep fans and competitors dry.

Tommy was returning to his rig from the arena when everything suddenly felt different. The energy around him was different. He wasn't superstitious—he had too much faith for that—but he did have a sixth sense his family called uncanny.

His brother Billy used to tease him he was like Spider Man, with the spidey tingle. Well, whatever it was, the sixth sense was tingling now, telling him something was up, and so when he turned the corner and spotted Dr. Blake Eden on her phone two hours from her home, he wasn't shocked.

Not completely.

But surprised enough, as he hadn't seen his wife in three years.

He was also intrigued. The fact Blake was here in Salinas meant she wasn't hiding from him anymore. She wasn't avoiding him. She'd come to deal with what they'd done. Good girl. He'd been ready for a long time.

Tommy walked toward Blake, footsteps muffled by the dirt. He was glad he wasn't competing until much later. No one wanted to climb on a pissed off bull right after a huge shock.

Fortunately, she hadn't seen him yet, too absorbed in her call, giving him time to study her, appreciate her.

His wife was, without a doubt, the most beautiful woman he'd ever seen, and that was saying something as every week he was at a rodeo or fairground where they were crowning a young, stunning beauty queen. Beautiful women trailed after him, slipping him their number, finding him at his hotel, or having a drink with his brother at a bar. But he wasn't interested in any of them. He only had eyes for Blake, and now, at long last, she was here.

His wife, the doctor.

From their first conversation, he'd been blown away by her mind and that face.

Clear light, green-gold eyes. High, prominent cheekbones balanced by full, lush lips.

Gold brown curls. Skin lightly bronzed, as if dusted with gold.

Her beauty had knocked him sideways, and then she'd thanked him for his help, and he was done. Her voice, low, husky, her diction… smart, educated, precise. Most cowboys would recognize they were outsmarted, outclassed, but he wasn't your average cowboy, either.

No, he hadn't gone to college, but he wasn't slow. His high school guidance counselor had called him in one day at the end of his junior year to say Tommy had scored perfectly on the SAT test, and what colleges was he applying to?

Tommy liked Mrs. Smith, she was a nice lady, always trying to help her students dream bigger, work harder, and so Tommy was polite as he told her he wasn't going to college. He was continuing as he had been, competing on the rodeo circuit. He was a cowboy. He liked being a cowboy. College wasn't for him.

She'd been so disappointed. Tommy was the brightest student Marietta had seen in years. How could he not avail himself of the scholarships and opportunities out there?

Sweet Mrs. Smith. He owed her a visit the next time he was home in Montana.

But now he had a visitor. A visitor he was very much looking forward to talking to.

So what if they'd only ever had three days together? So what if those days had been an intense, roller coaster?

For him, it had pretty much been love at first sight. He still loved her. He wouldn't have married her, and waited for her, if this wasn't the real thing. No one knew, either. His family didn't know. Her family didn't know. They'd had a secret marriage for years, and during this time, Tommy

Wyatt, rodeo champion, had been biding his time, waiting for her to make the next move. And now, finally, she had.

THE BABY HAIR on Blake's nape lifted.

She felt a shiver raced through her. She shifted the phone, looked around. He was here, wasn't he?

She glanced around again, and yes, there he was, standing in front of a beer truck, watching her. A veil of mist separated them, part fog, part drizzle, and she could feel the moisture in her curls, feel the wetness on her face. Suddenly her heart ached. She hadn't expected that.

"I have to go," she whispered to Kendrick, mouth drying, legs going weak. "He's here."

"Are you going to be okay?" Kendrick asked.

Kendrick was so good to her. "Yes," she said lowly, her chest growing tight. "I'll call soon." She ended the call and slipped the phone into her coat pocket and stared at the man who had turned her world inside out one December, making her want things she couldn't want.

Making her feel things she'd never felt before.

Making her take risks that she would have never taken otherwise.

The three years and three months since Las Vegas disappeared, fading into nothing, and she saw him just as she'd seen him that first night when he'd stepped between her and danger, protecting her from the bad guys. Protecting her from harm.

He'd saved her and smiled as if it had been nothing.

He'd kissed her gently on the cheek, despite the blood on his own.

"Hello, Tommy." She forced a smile, cold and hot shivers racing through her, her heart pounding so fast, too fast.

"You look beautiful."

A lump filled her throat. Just like the night she'd met him in the casino, he was wearing his black cowboy hat, and a thumb was hooked next to his big silver belt buckle. His jeans hugged his legs. He was even leaner than the last time she saw him, wide shoulders, deep chest, narrow hips, long strong legs. Thighs and glutes with impressive power.

Making love to him was earth shattering. Tommy loved her as if there was no tomorrow. He'd held her as if he would always be there to keep her safe. Whole.

No one would ever make her feel that way.

And just seeing him again made her miss what could have been. How she'd loved him those few days. How she'd wanted what she'd seen in his eyes.

His beautiful blue eyes met hers now and held.

"It's been a long time," he said.

She nodded, unable to speak. When she'd left him in Las Vegas three years ago, she'd promised him they'd soon be together. She'd promised him that she just needed a few days to break the news to her family, and then he'd join her, and she'd introduce him to them, and then they'd go to his family in Montana, and they'd do the same thing.

So Blake went home for her Christmas and he went home to his and they spoke almost every day. Every day he asked her, *Have you told your family yet?* And every day she had a reason why she hadn't. Her grandmother wasn't well, and her mom was taking care of her. Her dad was stressed with changes at work. Her dad's brother had just had a heart attack and was at the hospital. There were problems and worries and she didn't want to be a problem or a worry for her family. He said he understood. He told her, *wait, we can wait.*

*Take care of yourself,* he said.

*Take care of your family.*

So, she did, until the day came where her own blood test results revealed her greatest fear. Things were bad again.

She knew two things the day the doctor called to say she had to come in immediately, that it would be a hard fight. And that Tommy couldn't ever know.

Tommy Wyatt was handsome and wonderful—heroic in every sense of the word—but Blake's world was complicated and she didn't need a hero. She had to be her own hero. There was no room for marriage, or a man.

It was on January seventeenth she sent him a text, saying they made a mistake. They needed to acknowledge that they'd been impulsive, and foolish, and they needed to dissolve the marriage. Would he do it, since he lived in a state where divorce was fast and relatively easy if there was no contention, and there shouldn't be?

Tommy had answered her text with a text. *"I don't make a commitment and run from it."*

Frustrated she answered him. *"We don't even know each other!"*

*"It didn't seem to matter when we were together in December,"* he replied.

*"I want out,"* she texted back. She knew it sounded cold, but she was scared and panicked. She'd forgotten herself. She'd lost sight of her studies and her goals. Marriage wasn't part of her plan. It had to end, now. Maybe Tommy's parents wouldn't care that he'd done this, but her parents would be devastated. They'd feel betrayed. She married on a whim? She'd thrown caution to the wind? After all they'd done for her? After all they'd scrimped and sacrificed, leveraging everything—their home, their security—to send her to medical school.

She couldn't fail them. She couldn't disappoint them, not after everything they'd been through together these past ten years.

*"We can't do this by text,"* he answered hours later, hours where she'd been in agony because Tommy was a good person, Tommy was wonderful, and if circumstances had been different, he would be the one. He'd be everything.

She answered, blinking back tears. *"You want a phone call?"*

His text was immediate. *"No, we need to see each other. This has to be done face-to-face."*

Only she couldn't do that. If she'd seen him at that point, she wouldn't have been strong enough to leave him, and so she'd just let it go.

She pretended he didn't exist. She pretended they'd never promised each other forever.

"How long are you in town for?" he asked her.

"Just today. Will head back to the city tomorrow," she answered, referencing San Francisco where she was finishing her residency at San Francisco General Hospital and Trauma Center. She'd soon be done and was already interviewing for jobs. She hoped to stay in the Bay Area to be close to her parents, as well as the outstanding medical facilities there. The ideal job would be somewhere like San Mateo or East Palo Alto, but Blake was realistic and knew she'd probably have to commute.

"I take it you didn't come for the rodeo," he said, looking at her in a way no one but him ever looked at her. Protective. Hungry. Proud. Fierce.

Her insides did another quiver and she remembered how he'd held her. As if she were priceless. Irreplaceable.

She'd loved it, and him. Had desperately loved him.

The lump in her throat grew. It hurt to swallow. "You told me we had to do this in person. Face-to-face. So here I am."

"Smart of you to wait until I was in your neck of the woods, although I have been at the Cow Palace a couple of times since Vegas."

"It's been hectic with work. They'd said the days would be long. They weren't kidding."

"Do you really sleep at the hospital some nights?"

"When you're lucky enough to have an hour to rest, yes."

"How long until you're able to practice on your own?"

"I have to pass my boards, and earn my license, but I'm in a good place for both. I've been studying a lot, getting ready for the exam. Hoping by May or June I'll be done."

"That's impressive."

"General practice is a much shorter residency than being a surgeon."

"You should be proud of yourself. I'm very proud of you. But I never doubted you. You're going to be an exceptional doctor."

"Let's hope."

"No hoping. I have complete confidence in you. You are the smartest person I know. You are destined to do great things."

Her eyes burned. Heat washed through her, heat and that prickly awareness that made her feel raw, exposed. The fact that this big, tough guy—capable of fighting four guys at once—was always so good to her, so gentle with her, made her chest seize, her heart ache.

He deserved so much better. She knew it. He had to know it, too. She'd treated him poorly, pushing him away, thinking he'd finally let her go, walk away. He did the opposite. He dug in his heels and hung on. Like the rodeo star he was.

"We were impulsive, Tommy," she said huskily, burning with all the emotions she'd kept suppressed. "Who does what we did? Crazy people!"

"Or people crazy in love."

They had been. She had been. But she couldn't let him know it. "It was impractical. And we both regretted it—"

"I didn't."

Blake couldn't look at him. She didn't want to be swayed by his beautiful blue eyes, or his gorgeous face. She didn't want to let the pull of attraction weaken her resolve. "I did," she said, hoping God would forgive her for the lie. But if Tommy knew the truth, and had all the facts, he wouldn't divorce her, and she couldn't keep him tied to her any longer.

Tommy stayed silent.

She hated that he was going to make this hard, make her be the difficult one. She wasn't difficult. She wasn't demanding. She just wanted to fix a mistake that shouldn't have been made. "Tommy, I had so much fun being with you. It was all new and it was all exciting. You were a hero, rescuing me at the casino. You were fun, and smart, and I'd never met anyone like you. I still haven't. I loved spending those days with you, loved going to the arena and watching you take the All-Around title."

She looked at him, heart racing, feeling almost dizzy. "Those three days were like a fairy tale. They were an amazing fantasy. I was the princess, and you were the prince. But then I got home and I realize there are no fairy tales. There are no storybook endings." She swallowed around the lump in her throat. "I am not a princess, and you are not a prince. We're just two people that got caught up in something and you couldn't—wouldn't—let me go."

"I don't want to let you go."

"Why?"

"You're my girl."

This would kill her. But she had to resist him and his love and his endless charm. "We've spent no time together. We barely know each other."

"You're right. But at the same time, we promised to make it work, and we can't just give up because it's the easiest thing to do. I don't believe in divorce. Not for me. Not for us."

"I never thought I'd get divorced, but then, I never planned on getting married. I wish we'd been drinking and I could blame the wedding on alcohol, but I can't. So, I just have to assume I wasn't in my right mind. That we weren't—"

"I knew what I was doing. I wanted you. And I knew you were meant for me, even if we'd only just met."

"That's lust… infatuation."

"Or love."

"It can't be love! Real love doesn't happen in a flash. Real love is mature love. Real love takes time to grow."

"I come from a long line of romantics then. My grand-parents met at church and were married by the end of the month. My mom and dad fell in love over a weekend, while he was in Sacramento, competing in a rodeo. They were married a few months later and were together until he died. One of my brothers fell in love with someone practically at first glance. Love can happen quickly. But what makes a relationship work is the time you invest. That's what we have never done."

"Because I don't have time for a relationship. That's an-other issue, and a very real issue. How would we make this work? Who would give up their career? We live in different places, and we want different things. Tommy, come on. Don't make this more difficult than it already is. Just sign the papers!"

"Then we're giving up without trying. I'm not a quitter. I want us to give our marriage a chance before we give up. I'm not ready to give up."

She turned away, arms folded tightly over her chest. "I don't have to have your signature then," she said in a low voice. "I can file without you."

"But I can contest it."

"I know." She wouldn't look at him. "That's what I don't want. I want this clean… easy."

"Sweetheart, life isn't clean or easy."

"Don't I know that," Blake said under her breath, fury and frustration filling her.

He had no idea what she lived with. He had no idea who she was, or what she dealt with. Her life wasn't easy. Nothing had ever been handed to her. Only he didn't know that, because he didn't know the first thing about her. He'd been drawn to her face, and her legs, and maybe her smile. He liked her humor and her intelligence, but those were all surface things. He only knew the most superficial things about her, and it wasn't enough to make a relationship work. It certainly wasn't enough to make a marriage work.

She faced him. "How can you want to stay married to me, when you know I don't want to be with you?"

For a long moment there was just silence, and then he shrugged his broad shoulders, expression almost mocking. "Because I know how you felt when we were together in Las Vegas. You wanted. You needed me. You couldn't get enough of me. And even if it was crazy and impulsive, we thought life would be better together."

He was right. Every word he said was true. She'd wanted him, and needed him, and she'd never wanted to let him go. But that was her running away from life, running away from reality. Their weekend was just an escape from the real world, not the real world.

"Maybe we did exchange vows in a tacky little chapel off the Strip," he added flatly, "but they were vows made to each other before God, and despite everything that has happened since, I take those vows seriously."

They weren't getting anywhere and she could tell she was

just getting Tommy's back up. He was tough, tenacious, and the last thing she wanted was a fight. If this turned into a fight, it'd be awful, and she didn't want him as her adversary.

Not when she still had so many feelings for him.

"Can we talk tonight, when you're done?" she asked, digging her hands into her coat pockets, fighting to stay calm. Collected. Which wasn't easy when just standing close to Tommy made her heart race and her legs unsteady. The man was still so hot and potent. She didn't think she'd ever be close to him and immune, which was why she'd kept her distance all these years. Tommy Wyatt was dangerous. He was her own personal kryptonite.

"Alright," he said, his voice deep, husky.

He had a beautiful voice. She'd missed his voice. Missed those intense blue eyes. Missed his big shoulders and broad chest and how, when he held her, she'd felt so safe, untouchable. The world couldn't reach her. Problems couldn't hurt her. In his arms, she knew no one and nothing would get her.

"Be careful," she said. "Out there."

"I'll do my best."

"Don't take unnecessary risks—"

"I never do."

She laughed in disbelief. "You always do. Every night you compete."

"I'm good at what I do. Don't worry about me."

*But I do*, she thought, her gaze intently studying his face, memorizing the lean planes of his cheeks, the firm mouth, the square chin.

Her colleagues called her the doctor of titanium and ice, claimed she had nerves of steel, an unshakeable focus and resolve. It wasn't true. It was all a front. Beneath her tough exterior, was doubt and loneliness. But only Tommy knew that side of her. He was the only person who'd gotten behind her walls, storming them with his passion and humor, completely stealing her heart.

He'd loved her, and he'd made her laugh, and then he'd loved her some more. With him in Las Vegas she'd laughed until she cried. And every night in Las Vegas, she'd held him, held tightly onto him, as if the world was ending, and in hindsight, it was.

"Should I put you on the pass list?" he asked. "Or are you going to be studying somewhere?"

She had planned on returning to her hotel room and studying. She'd planned on keeping her distance, making sure he didn't get close and chip away at her armor, but seeing him now, she desperately wanted to see him in ride, rope, be the champion cowboy he was. "I can buy my own ticket," she said.

He smiled slowly, his gaze heating. "I'll put you on the list, and I'll find you after."

"YOU OKAY?" BILLY asked his brother as they stretched,

staying warm before the opening ceremonies.

Tommy nodded. "Why?"

"You seem pretty distracted." Billy nodded at one of the bull fighters walking by before looking back at his brother. "Like there's something on your mind. Which is never good before you ride."

Tommy did have a lot on his mind, and Billy was right. Going into the bronc riding with too many thoughts wasn't the ideal scenario, but after seeing Blake earlier, he hadn't been able to think of anything but her. The curve of her cheek. The gold of her eyes. The honey bronze of her skin. He remembered how her lips felt, and how addictive she was in his bed.

Lovemaking had been tender, passionate, sweet. It had been the best sex he'd ever known, not because it was erotic, but because it had been emotional. He'd wanted her in a way he'd never wanted anyone—desiring to know her, and love her, all of her. He'd been fully present, and she'd felt so alive, so responsive. He wasn't performing for her, he was simply loving her, and it was the easiest, best thing, he'd ever done.

Leaving her was hard, almost impossible, and he'd arrived late at the stadium on the next to last night. Normally he'd be there early on a Friday, going through his routine but he'd lost track of time, and when he finally looked at his watch, he knew he was in trouble, in more ways than one. On his way to the Thomas Mack arena he checked his phone. Billy had called. Sam had called. Other friends had called. Everyone was calling, wanting to know where he was. If he was okay. Wanting to know if he needed help.

Billy left a series of messages, saying he had Tommy's horses and clothes for him, but call.

*Call.*

Tommy sent a text. *"All good. On the way."*

He wouldn't panic, but he knew he'd cut it far too close. If it weren't for his brothers and sister-in-law, he wouldn't have been able to ride. But Billy and Sam had warmed up his horses. He had clean clothes. He arrived, stretched, was ready to go.

Tommy had come to the National Finals Rodeo to win, and he was going to win. Every night mattered. The points mattered. He had a chance to earn the All-Around title this year, and he wanted it. It helped that Billy and Sam were competing with him, and against him. It had been a great year for the Wyatts, and they'd all made the finals. The Wyatt brothers had grown up competitive, but also supportive of each other, and if he wasn't going to win, he wanted Sam or Billy to win.

But this year, he was winning.

This year he was leaving Vegas as world champion.

Blake did show that night. He spotted her where a guest would be. She'd come on her own—and he wondered what her friends thought. She stayed until the end. Sam's wife was able to give Blake a message, letting Blake know Tommy would take her home after, if she just waited.

Blake waited, leaving with him later.

He'd introduced her briefly to his brothers, told them he'd see them at one of the parties, but they never made it to the parties. They went back to his trailer, and stayed in his trailer the next day, practically all day, until it was time to return to the arena for the final night, Saturday night's competition.

He ended Saturday night as the All-Around cowboy, and by morning, he was also a married man.

He never told his brothers about the wedding at the little chapel. He'd vowed to wait until Blake told her family, and then they'd break the news to his family together.

It never happened.

Tommy crossed to the curtains separating the arena into a smaller space for the rodeo events. The Salinas rodeo was over a hundred years old, the first stadium built in 1911, and normally he liked competing here, but he was distracted.

He searched the stands for her, scanning sections, and rows, until he finally saw her, not far from the bull chutes.

Ten rows from the bottom, middle of the section. Empty seats on either side of her. She sat by herself, a program on her lap.

She was looking away from him, watching something in the distance.

Her curls were pulled back in a high ponytail, showing off her stunning cheekbones and full mouth. She was still the most beautiful woman he had ever seen in his life and for three days she had been his. He wouldn't say those were the best days of his life, because those three days had been intense, a roller coaster of ups and downs, and love. He'd fallen for her hard and fast, and when they were together, it made sense. But when he was away from her, he questioned his sanity. What in heaven's name was he doing? He wasn't a romantic. He'd certainly never gone looking for love, not wanting entanglements when he was focused on work. On winning.

But he'd fallen for her anyway.

Billy joined him at the curtain, looking out at the stands, trying to see what Tommy was seeing. "So the distraction is out there," Billy said.

Tommy glanced at his brother. "My life really isn't that interesting."

Billy just smiled. "You're the last to go. We're all interested in what you find interesting."

"You make marriage sound like a trap."

"Not at all. We just want you happy. *I* want you happy."

"I am."

Billy stilled, leaned closer to Tommy, craning to see past him. "Is that who I think it is?"

Tommy closed his eyes, praying they weren't talking about the same person. "Who?"

"The girl from Vegas. Can't remember her name. Adam and Eve… Eve from Eden."

So Billy had seen her. And Billy remembered her. Not

good. Billy was like a dog with a bone. He never let things go. "Blake," Tommy said casually. "Eden," he added. "And yes, she's here. Drove down from San Francisco."

Billy prodded him. "Don't act like you don't care. She's hot. Probably too hot for you."

"She's smart. Too smart for you."

"Touché. So, you're going to get lucky tonight? You've been celibate way too long. Or are you going to say she's just a friend?"

"You're worse than a kid. I feel sorry for your wife."

Billy grinned. "I love your non-answer answer. You've always been so good at that."

"What? Being discreet?" Tommy forced himself to relax. He had to relax. The last thing he wanted was to get stomped on or rolled on during his first event. In front of her, no less. "Blake's a doctor. She's just finishing her residency."

"Seriously? Good for her."

"Yeah. It's good to see her." Understatement of the year.

"Have her come to dinner with us. I'd like to congratulate her."

"We'll see." Tommy dropped the curtain and turned around, gaze sweeping the pens with horses and cattle. He smacked his hands together, energy building, excitement and nerves making his pulse quicken. "Let's do this. I could use some points tonight."

❦

BLAKE SAT IN the stands, hands knotted in her lap. She probably didn't need that extra espresso. She was already wound up tight. The coffee was just giving her jitters now.

She wasn't nervous for Tommy. He was good. But oh, the injuries in his sport were horrendous. There were deaths, too, but she didn't want to think about that. She just wanted Tommy to do well and then get him to sign the paperwork she'd brought with her and hopefully they could part on good terms. Because, otherwise, it'd be unbearable. She didn't hate him. It was just the opposite. She cared. Too much. But they were too different, and their goals were too different. He was a country boy. She had been raised in the city. He frequently broke things. She was forever mending things. He was an optimist. She was a realist. Yes, opposites could attract, but life was too grueling, too challenging, to hitch one's wagon to another on a whim.

And there he was.

On the bars of the chute, checking the ropes, making sure everything was secure.

Her heart raced at the sight of him. Broad shouldered, lean, tan, strong. He'd looked older when she saw him outside the stadium this afternoon. He had new creases at his eyes, and grooves near his mouth as if he didn't smile as much as he used to. Maybe she was being fanciful, but she worried about him. She'd worried a lot these past three years. Was he okay? Was he riding well? Had he gotten hurt? Was he seeing someone else?

She hadn't wanted to think about him, though. She honestly tried hard not to.

Due to school, studying, and family demands, she didn't have the luxury of thinking about him endlessly, and with time, she did think of him less. There was one long period where she wasn't well and at home, recovering. During those days she'd missed him terribly, and everything in her wanted to reach out to him. She would have given anything to hear his voice.

To hear him say her name.

To have him make her laugh, or at the very least, tease her so she'd smile.

She missed the pitch of his voice, and the way he spoke, and the way he listened.

She missed him.

But she didn't reach out, she couldn't, it would just mean starting everything up again, and that was the one thing that couldn't happen.

Time continued to help. School helped. Applying for her residency helped. Focusing on moving forward helped.

And then something would happen and it'd knock her back.

It always was something outside herself that brought the memories back—the pair of boots in a store window, the commercial with horses on TV, the handsome blond actor in a movie—and she'd flash back to the time she had her own handsome cowboy, and the emotion would fill her, the emotion overwhelming.

He wasn't hers, though. She'd given him up.

Kendrick had only recently entered the picture as a romantic option, and while she didn't feel romantic feelings for him, and they'd never had a date, his presence in her life gave her the courage to come here today and make the break.

And she would make the break, if it was the last thing she did.

# CHAPTER TWO

IT WASN'T TOMMY'S best night, but it wasn't his worst. He didn't get kicked or stomped on, nor did he get thrown too hard. His bull gave him a low score, but the re-ride helped, so now he just had to wait for tomorrow night and hope he performed better so he'd be there Sunday afternoon for the finals.

He had time between events to think about Billy's suggestion that Blake join them for dinner. At first, Tommy was a no, but the more he thought about it, the more brilliant the idea appeared. If they all went to dinner, it would prolong the evening, giving Tommy a chance to spend more time with Blake. He knew she wanted to rush in and rush out, but the last thing he wanted was his wife rushing away.

He needed time with her. Time to convince her they hadn't made a mistake; that their marriage could work if they just tried. They'd never tried. And he didn't fault Blake. He couldn't imagine going to med school. He couldn't imagine being a resident physician. He couldn't imagine the long hours, or the endless hours studying. He couldn't imagine the stress. He wouldn't want any of the stress. But he did want her.

Just seeing her earlier made him feel everything. He wished he knew why she was the one for him. He didn't know why she was the one. But she was.

Since meeting her, he was interested in no one else, and it wasn't just because they married. He could have divorced her. He could have moved forward. But he wasn't ready to let it end. He wasn't going to lose her without a fight. She was worth the fight. She was worth everything.

And maybe she didn't feel that way about him, but that was okay. She didn't have to feel that way right now. They'd known each other three days. They'd spent three years apart. Clearly what was missing was a relationship.

They'd never done the usual dating, wooing, falling in love thing.

They'd jumped headfirst into forever, which in hindsight wasn't smart, but they'd done it and he was going to do his best to keep the woman he loved.

Before he signed anything, he was going to tell her he deserved a chance. A real one. But those words would be easier to say, and maybe easier to hear, after a decent dinner. A good meal cured many ills, or so his mother liked to say, and Tommy tended to respect his mother.

So tonight they'd go have dinner, and they'd sit down and visit like adults. They needed to be grown-ups, have some civilized conversation, maybe a beer, a few laughs. Dinner with Billy would be fun. Billy was fun. Billy was easygoing. Not as handsome or charming as Tommy, but he came close.

But after the rodeo ended and Tommy suggested dinner to Blake, she was not enthusiastic.

"I don't want to go to dinner," she said. "I just want to talk to you. I can't talk to you if we're at dinner with you brother."

"Let's be civilized. Have a meal, visit a little bit. You weren't going to drive back to San Francisco until tomorrow, and you need to eat. So join us, and then you and I can talk after."

DINNER WAS NICE. She couldn't find fault with Tommy or Billy. They were good company—clever, interesting, handsome, witty. Billy told stories about his son, a little boy who started riding a horse before he could even walk. He had a nice place in Utah which made it convenient for stops while on the circuit.

Now that she thought about it, Billy had done most of the talking. Tommy had just watched her, his piercing blue eyes studying her intently.

Maybe she should have sat next to Tommy instead of across from him.

No, that would have been worse.

She just needed to escape. Maybe once outside, her head wouldn't ache so much. Maybe fresh air—and space—would help. She'd started a new medicine a week ago and headaches and queasiness were one of the most common side effects. Her body would eventually adjust. It always did.

Outside the restaurant, she said goodbye to Billy. She and Tommy were silent as they walked to his truck. He glanced at her as he climbed behind the steering wheel. "You okay?"

"Head hurts," she admitted. "But it's okay."

"Need something for the pain?"

"Do you have something?"

He opened the console between them and pulled out a bottle of ibuprofen. "Two?" he asked, snapping the lid off. "Three?"

"Three, please."

He drew an unopened water bottle from the side of his door, twisted off the cap, and handed it to her. "Has it been bothering you all night?" he asked, after she'd washed down the pills.

She gave her head the smallest of shakes. "It wasn't too bad at first, but the last half hour got a little rough."

"You should have told me."

"You and Billy were having a good time."

"We always have a good time. Next time speak up."

They drove in silence. She kept her eyes closed, trying to breathe deep, knowing she needed to relax. The medicine would kick in faster that way. The restaurant wasn't far from her hotel, but even so, Blake was grateful Tommy left the radio off. But in the silence, she wondered if he played music a lot, or what he listened to. Did he prefer country music? Did he like rap or rock? She didn't know, couldn't remember. There was so much she didn't know about him, just as there were important things he didn't know about her. She'd kept things from him. Not because she'd wanted to deceive him, but because her time with him in Las Vegas had been an escape.

It had been their time. Perfect. Surreal.

It wasn't until she returned to California she realized they should have talked more, made love less.

She should have shared things. She owed him that much, didn't she? But she hadn't wanted to see his expression change. She didn't want him to turn away. How much better to just live in the moment... wild, free. To live the way she'd always wanted to be.

Back in her San Francisco apartment, she was still on a high, still in heaven, still savoring their three perfect days. The high continued throughout the holidays, and she was going to tell her parents. She fully intended to tell everyone. But her grandmother's flu turned into pneumonia and for a couple weeks there, her condition was precarious, and then her dad lost his job the day after Christmas, and New Year's was grim. She'd never seen her dad cry, but she walked into the kitchen and found him with tears in his eyes as he stood before the coffee machine, contemplating yet another day, unemployed. For the first time in his adult life, he had no work, nowhere to go.

That very same night her dad's brother had a heart attack.

And then her bloodwork came back, followed by a CT scan.

That was when reality set in. She'd been playing... dreaming... she couldn't stay married. It didn't work for them to be married.

Blake didn't block Tommy from her mind. She did the opposite. She lived and relived the days, the hours, the love, until she couldn't because it'd drive her mad.

Life wasn't fair. And life didn't care who it hit, or broke. So Blake sent him a message it was over, and then did the only thing she could—put her head down, and focused on getting by. One painful day at a time.

Tommy braked, and his hand lightly brushed her arm. "We're almost there," he said, his voice deep, a husky rasp.

She sat up and opened her eyes. "That was fast."

"You were sleeping."

"Just resting," she said, glad to be back, looking forward to her cool, dark room.

Pulling into reception, Tommy shifted into park. "Can I walk you up?"

She shook her head. "I'll be fine." Blake gathered her purse and coat. "I know we were supposed to talk, but—"

"Tomorrow's fine," he interrupted. "Want to call me when you're awake? Let me know how you feel?"

She squirmed. "I don't have your number anymore."

"I'll send it again."

"I blocked you." Blake glanced at him, grimaced. "I'm sorry."

He dug around his console, retrieved a Sharpie and a glossy postcard—of him—used at his signing events. Tommy quickly jotted down his number and gave her the card. "Now you have it. Call me when you're feeling up to talking."

"Okay."

"If your head gets worse, let me know. I'll get you help, take you to a doctor."

She smiled crookedly, amused. "I am a doctor but thank you."

He came around to her side, opened the door, and gave her his hand, assisting her down since it was a high step. "I've got an appearance at the mall at noon, which will take an hour or so, but am free before, and free after. Just let me know."

"I should feel better in the morning. Want to do coffee?"

"I'm more of a breakfast guy, and there's a good breakfast place across the street. You can have coffee, your slice of wheat toast, and two egg whites scrambled with spinach and feta."

He remembered. Well, she remembered his breakfast, too. "And you can order four scrambled eggs, hash browns crispy, three strips of bacon—crispy, two sausages well done, and a stack of buckwheat pancakes." She lifted a brow, feeling as if she'd trumped him. "*With* extra butter and syrup."

"Good memory."

She waved the card with his image and number. "I'll text you when I wake up."

"See you tomorrow."

She was just letting herself into her room when her phone rang. She closed the door, locked it, before fishing her phone from her purse and answering. It was Kendrick. "Hi."

"I hadn't heard from you. Got worried," he said.

"It's just been a long day."

"You okay?"

"I have a pretty nasty headache but I've taken something and a good sleep will help."

"It's the new medicine, isn't it?"

"Yes. So far not a fan."

"Hang in there," he said.

"I'm trying."

Kendrick cleared his throat. "So, have you had a chance to talk to Tom?"

"Not really. His brother is here so it's challenging getting him alone. But he and I are going to meet for coffee in the morning and hopefully that will be that."

"It must be stressful. I should have gone with you."

"It's good you didn't. It would only make things harder." Blake sat down on the edge of the bed, and eased her half boots off, one, and then the other. "I've got this. I do."

"What time did you think you'll be back?"

"Not sure. Early afternoon probably."

"Are we still having dinner with my parents? I know they're looking forward to meeting you but I don't want to put pressure on you."

Blake hadn't forgotten, but suddenly the idea of dinner with anyone, much less such an important I-want-you-to-meet-my-parents dinner overwhelmed her. Kendrick was a friend. She was afraid he was beginning to push things, move too fast. "We might need to reschedule," she said.

"I hope not. They're excited about dinner."

"I'll call you tomorrow," she said, now also queasy and filled with dread. If Kendrick hadn't helped her so much in school, if he hadn't studied with her when she was sick then maybe she wouldn't feel obliged to meet his parents, and accept a date. "Good night."

"Good night. Feel better."

Hanging up, Blake lay back on the bed and looked up at the ceiling, blinking hard, holding all the emotion in.

Her feelings for Kendrick were complicated. He was her friend, first, a fellow med student, and then a late-night study buddy, and finally, a best friend. He and her parents were the ones who got her through the tough times. He'd never asked for anything… until lately.

She wasn't quite in love with him, but she cared for him. She didn't want to hurt him. Why, oh why, did he have to confess his feelings for her?

Why couldn't they have remained close friends... buddies?

Blake reached up, rubbed her forehead and then tugged on her ear trying to ease the pain.

Her head still throbbed, but now her heart hurt, too.

Blake hadn't thought she'd sleep well, but she woke early, headache gone, emotions calm. She climbed from bed, did some of her favorite simple yoga-based stretches before making coffee with her room coffeemaker. While the coffee brewed, she pulled out some books she'd brought, as she always had reading and research to do.

Normally, she was disciplined but this morning she couldn't settle and read, not when thoughts of Tommy kept intruding.

She could see him so clearly, in his blue denim shirt, tight Wranglers and the protective vest he wore during his bronc and bull riding events. When he went sailing across the ring last night, hat flying, he managed to land on his feet and the smile he gave the cheering fans as he straightened took her breath away. He didn't take himself too seriously. His smile was beautiful. The man was gorgeous. And the way he walked... wow.

Wow.

Kendrick was brilliant, and kind, and so good to her, but Tommy was like lightning—he lit her up, made her feel, made her feel new.

She didn't want to compare them. She couldn't compare them, but oh, this was hard. Her calm was deserting her. She needed to just do this, get the divorce petition signed, and head home. Tommy was Tommy, world champion cowboy, a winner. He wouldn't be down long. People like Tommy always came out on top. He didn't need her. She wasn't essential to his world. Whereas Kendrick lived and breathed medicine. They had the same interests and passions, and if she could fall in love with Kendrick, they could make a great team.

But Blake had only ever loved one man, and that was Tommy.

She didn't fall in love easily, and she knew she was kidding herself if she thought she'd develop romantic feelings for Kendrick.

But he was a catalyst for change. His declaration of love for her made her realize she had to get the divorce handled. She couldn't remain secretly married forever.

Blake grabbed her phone and the five-by-seven card featuring Tommy. She studied him a long moment—the pose, the confidence, the half smile. Tommy might appear laidback, but he had fast reflexes and impressive control. His eight seconds on that bull last night only reinforced that impression.

*Time to see him. Time to get this done.* She texted Tommy. *"Want to meet at the Country Café at nine?"*

*"I'll pick you up,"* he answered promptly.

*"It's across the street,"* she replied.

*"So?"*

Blake rolled her eyes. She wasn't going to argue with him about that. There were bigger things on her mind. *"Fine. I'll be outside the hotel at nine."*

He was there when she stepped out of the hotel doors. She walked to his truck and he started to step out but she didn't wait for him to open her door. Blake opened the passenger door herself, climbed in. "Good morning," she said.

He looked and smelled as if he'd just stepped from the shower, fresh, clean, lightly scented with something masculine and oh-so appealing. "How is your head?"

"Good. Pain is gone."

"I'm glad. I was worried about you."

She gave him an amused side glance. "It was just a headache, handsome."

He flashed her a grin. "Am I handsome?"

Blake laughed, and then shook her head, because he had a way of making her laugh, making her feel free… happy. "You're ridiculous."

"Thank you."

Her gaze met his as he shifted into drive. The intensity in his expression sent a jolt through her. It wasn't simply heat, but… longing. Desire. Need.

A lump filled her throat and she turned away, looked out the window, eyes stinging. She did care for him—*love him*, a little voice challenged on the inside.

She'd always cared for him—*loved him*, the little voice repeated.

But that didn't mean they worked in real life. She needed him to agree. That was the challenge.

There was a brief wait at the restaurant to be seated but then they had a big yellow vinyl booth in the back near a window. The walls were a paneled oak with lots of framed photos and posters of past rodeos and local cowboys and barrel racers. *No wonder Tommy likes this place*, Blake thought as the waitress came by and filled their coffee cups.

She took their order then, too, since Tommy was hungry and then after she was gone, Tommy looked Blake in the eyes. "So why now?" he asked bluntly. "Besides the whole residency is ending and I'm going to be getting a job somewhere soon?"

She added a splash of cream to her coffee, needing the diversion since it was impossible to think clearly when he looked at her so directly. "That's not enough?"

"We both know there's plenty you're not saying." And then he smiled.

Blake didn't trust his smile. Tommy looked charming. Handsome. Relaxed. But she knew better. "I can't just want to move forward?"

He stretched his arm over the back of the booth, fingers tapping the vinyl, once, twice. "You look good. You're not as thin as when I last saw you."

"I'd been working really hard when we met. There

wasn't a lot of time to sleep or eat in those days."

"The bachelorette trip to Vegas should have been relaxing." His smile deepened, creases fanning from his eyes. "But then you met me. We didn't sleep much, did we?"

She smiled at him, her calm, collected smile, the one she offered patients who were difficult, disrespectful, not trusting that she, a young woman, could be a good doctor. "Why wouldn't you sign the divorce papers? I asked you repeatedly."

"You never asked me."

"I did."

"*No.* You never called. You never once spoke to me. You just mailed papers to me in a big old envelope, and then when I didn't sign those, you mailed me more. Regularly. What? Every six months? Nine months?"

"Nine months," she agreed. "But you never once responded."

"I wasn't going to do anything until we did this. Sit down and talked."

"As friends?" She heard her sarcasm but couldn't help it. He'd made everything more difficult than it needed to be.

"No, not as friends. We're not friends. Friends talk to each other. Friends communicate. A manila envelope to the ranch wasn't communication."

"Tommy, the bottom line is that it's time I moved forward, but I can't, not if I'm married to you."

"There's someone else, isn't there?" he asked.

Her breath caught, and she swallowed her surprise. She hadn't planned on talking about this, or mentioning Kendrick. "That's complicated."

"I'd think it's a yes or no answer."

"Yes," she said after a moment. "There is someone." It was a lie but maybe that's what she had to do. Lie to him. Swing at him. Push him away. "He's a doctor I've known for years," she added. "We were in med school together. He was able to get his residency at UCSF, so we're both still in San Francisco."

"Do you live together?"

"No."

"But you're together?"

"No. Not like that. No dates. We haven't been intimate." She gave him a pointed look. "I'm married, Tommy. I'm not out dating people, kissing people, but…"

"You'd like to be."

"You and I haven't seen each other in three years."

"I've wanted to see you."

She swallowed hard. It wouldn't help to get into a war of words. It wouldn't help to argue or protest. She just needed to stay focused and get the papers in her purse signed. Finally.

"Why could he see you, and I couldn't?" Tommy persisted.

"I didn't 'see' him. We were in classes together. We were studying together. We weren't romantic. It's only recently

I've realized—" She broke off, thinking she'd said too much.

Tommy just waited, expression blank, but his jaw was hard. She could see the tight pull of muscle. Feel his tension. He wasn't as relaxed as he was pretending.

"He's been there for me, Tommy. And he cares for me—"

"I care for you."

"But you and I, we're not compatible. Our goals aren't compatible. We shouldn't be together."

"But we are."

She closed her eyes, counted to five, and then ten. She couldn't let herself get upset. Nothing good would come of drama. "Kendrick—"

"That's his name?"

She nodded. "He's interested in neurosurgery, so he has another four years of his residency fellowship."

"Which is why you want to stay in San Francisco?"

"That, and because I want to stay close to my parents. We lost my grandmother a year ago. My dad's brother had a stroke after his heart attack and isn't quite as mobile. My parents aren't getting younger, either. It's important I stay close to them."

"Has Kendrick met them?"

She shook her head. "We're not together as in *together*, Tommy. We can't be, because I'm still married to you. But Kendrick has been really good to me. He's been there for me. And the logical next step is…"

"Marriage?"

"*No.* Dating. Possibilities. He wants me to meet his parents."

"Do you want to meet his parents?"

She sighed. "That's not the point."

"Does he know about me?" Tommy persisted.

"Not exactly, but yes, sort of."

"Well, that clears everything up."

She smiled faintly. She liked Tommy's humor. She always had. "Kendrick knows I made a promise of sorts to you. He knows I'm here, trying to handle the promise."

"What does he think this promise is?"

"Not marriage," she said, sighing.

"But I thought he was such a good friend?"

"*No one* knows I married, Tommy. And after all these years of being friends, and growing closer, it's not like I can just suddenly spring it on him, *'Hey, I have a husband, one I don't see, but yes I've been married all this time. Surprise!'*"

"Why not? I'd love to see his face when you break that news."

"I'm not going to tell him, at least, not right now, not if I don't have to. I suppose at some point I will tell him, not because we're a couple, but because he's my friend."

"A good friend."

"My best friend," she said, chin lifting slightly. "Women can have men as friends."

Tommy regarded her for a long moment. "Will he mind, you think, finding out you were married?"

"I would hope not."

"That's not a very encouraging answer."

"He comes from a conservative Christian family. Divorce is frowned upon in his family."

Tommy sipped his coffee. "He's told you this?"

"Yes."

"I think you need to tell him, sweetheart, sooner than later. Just because trust is a huge thing. If you love him—"

"I don't love him," she interrupted. "I like him. But he's made me realize I'm living a lie and I need to fix this. We need to fix this."

"You're worried about him, and his feelings, but what about me?" Tommy said, smiling at her. "Where do I factor into all this?"

He didn't have all the college education she did, but he was smart. Very smart. "I'd think you'd want to be free to pursue whatever opportunities are out there for you."

"You'd be wrong," he said.

He didn't add more as the waitress arrived with plates stacked on her arms. Eggs, and more eggs, toast, pancakes, and a platter of meat just for Tommy.

Blake was glad they let the discussion drop so they could eat while the food was hot, but in her mind, she was formulating thoughts, arguments, which she shared as soon as they were both done, as she wanted Tommy's full attention.

"Tommy, we haven't lived together, or seen each other in three years. We *never* lived together. We had a few days together, and I think we can both admit that we were stupid, impulsive, and in a moment of stupid and impulsive, we did something crazy. I have regretted it ever since. *Please* release me from this relationship. It's something I regret with my whole heart."

"I wasn't drunk when we said our vows. You weren't drunk either."

"Maybe not on alcohol, but on feel-good chemicals like oxytocin and dopamine. I was drunk on you, high from the rush of endorphins—"

"Oh, come on, Blake. I can't buy that, and neither should you. We didn't even make love until *after* we'd married."

"We didn't have to make love to feel high on you. The way you kissed me and smiled at me. The way you held me. Hugged me. Looked at me. Tommy, it all felt so magical, but it wasn't real—"

"How wasn't it real?"

"We have nothing in common. We have wildly different backgrounds. Wildly different goals."

"And yet, here we are, still married."

"We're still married because we've both been really busy. I didn't have time to chase you down until now. And I don't know why you haven't chased me down."

"That's not true. I did come looking for you."

"What? When?"

The waitress appeared, placed the bill on the table between them. Tommy took it, and returned it to the waitress without even looking, along with several folded green twenty-dollar bills.

"In March. Just about three years ago today. I went to your house. I spoke with your dad."

"You talked to Dad?"

"He's about six feet, two hundred and twenty pounds, muscular guy, keeps his hair shaved close, not super friendly." He looked at her. "Sound about right?"

"He was a military guy," she said.

"I figured as much. Your dad didn't invite me in. We talked on the front porch. He wanted to know what I wanted from you."

Blake was amazed by all this. "What did you tell him?"

"I certainly didn't say I was looking for my wife. Didn't think that would go down well."

"No, it wouldn't have." She exhaled. "I'm shocked."

"I wanted to find you, not them, but I couldn't find your address. I did find theirs. I'd hoped they'd tell me where you were, hoped…" He shook his head. "I don't know what I hoped. I hoped you'd be there. I hoped you'd walk out and you'd be happy to see me. I hoped we could at least talk. But your dad was definitely on the hostile side—"

"I told you."

"Your mom was nervous."

"That's Mom. She was probably afraid Dad would get upset, have a heart attack like Uncle Marcus."

"I wasn't there to wreck your life, so I just said I was an old friend, and asked your dad to let you know Tom Wyatt had come by."

She gave her head the smallest of shakes. "He didn't. And Mom didn't."

"I wondered."

The waitress returned with change, but Tommy said it was for her. He glanced over at Blake. "Ready to go?"

She nodded and they walked out of the café, into the sunlight. There was no mist or rain today. The sky was blue and the sun was bright.

But Blake wasn't ready to get into Tommy's truck. She didn't want to be cooped up. She faced him in the parking lot, outside the truck. "Tom, you're a good person. A really good person. I have nothing against you, but we're not meant to be together. We're so different, and we have different things we want, and I don't see how we fit into each other's lives."

"But your Kendrick does."

"We want the same things. We understand each other's work and each other's goals. We will be able to support each other in a way that you can't really support me and I can't support you. I should have thought of all that three years ago, I shouldn't have lost my head when I met you, but you caught me off guard. You surprised me. I forgot who I was and who I was supposed to be."

"Obviously not a cowboy's wife."

That hurt, and she didn't even know why. "Tom, I fix things. I fix people. You are in a job where you break things. You take horrific risks. You spend your life getting destroyed—"

"There are only a couple events that are truly dangerous."

"And those are the ones you excel in."

"I've been lucky."

"But luck doesn't last forever. Life doesn't last forever. You live on the road and are in a different town every weekend. That's not my life. And I don't want to be part of your rodeo life."

"If you said, *Tom, I want to be together. I want to live together, and have a family*, I'd retire tomorrow."

"Tommy."

"I mean it. If being settled in one spot is that important to you, I'd give it all up."

"And you'd leave Montana to come live in the Bay Area?"

"There are ranches in California. Property north of you, property south of you—"

"But that's not where I'll be working. And not where my parents live. I need to be in the city, or close to the city."

"Doctors are needed everywhere."

"True, but my parents—"

"They can't come live near you? You don't have brothers or sisters. You told me that when we met."

"My uncle—"

"Oh, come on, what about you? What about what's good for you? What about what's good for us?"

"But this is what I mean when I say we're not right for each other. There is someone waiting for you that is right for you. She loves small towns and wants to have lots of babies. I don't want babies—"

"You don't?"

She shook her head. "I'm not planning on being a mom."

Tommy stared at her dumbfounded. "You never said that before."

"I don't think we ever discussed children. Why would we? We were too busy kissing and staring into each other's eyes, living briefly in this alternate universe. It was all a fantasy. We weren't even dealing remotely with reality."

"Why don't you want kids?"

"I'd rather focus on work. On healing people."

"There's no reason you can't do both."

"I don't want to do both, Tommy. I know my limitations. I've studied medicine because I have a passion, a mission, and that's what I want to do."

"And Kendrick supports this?"

"Kendrick wants whatever is best for me."

"Sounds like a pushover."

"Just because he's not asserting his will over me?"

"I've never once asserted my will—"

"You are, now." She saw his expression and her stomach

cramped. "I don't want to hurt you, Tommy. You're the last person I want to hurt. Please don't make me say mean things. That's not why I'm here. I want us to part on good terms. I want to remember you as my own angel. My very own hero."

He said nothing and she felt the chasm between them grow. Every word she said just made him pull away. "We're not enemies," she said softly. "You're not the bad guy. I'm not a bad guy. But we have to be adults—"

"I've honored our vows, too," he said, quietly, a rasp in his deep voice. "Since I met you there has been no one else."

She looked away, heartsick. Every minute with him just felt worse. She felt worse. "Free me, Tommy, please. Just sign the papers. I have them with me. Sign them and it's over. We'll never have to have this conversation again."

"But I can't," he said. "I won't."

"Why not?"

"You haven't given me an equal chance. You disappeared and closed the door, leaving no room for me. I could agree to the divorce if I felt as if we'd tried, and failed, but to just give up because it's the easiest thing? That's wrong. Sweetheart, that's not me."

"So what do you want?"

"I want time with you. I want a year… a month."

"That's impossible. I'm still in residency until end of May. I have exams to take—"

"I'll leave the circuit, come live with you in the city."

That would most definitely not work. "You can't come to me. Besides, I'm never at home. I practically live at the hospital.".

"Then come with me. Give me one week. No work, no excuses."

"I—" Seeing his hard expression she broke off. He wasn't just going to let her go. He wanted something from her, and she understood that. "I don't know if that's possible, either. You have to put in for vacation weeks in advance—"

"We're not waiting weeks, or months. We're figuring this out now. I want you to give me the next week. All week. And if, at the end, you're still determined to divorce, I'll sign the papers and six months from then, you'll be free."

"We'll be free," she corrected.

"So you agree?"

She glanced at her watch, checked the time. It was nearing eleven. He had an appearance coming up. She'd planned on driving home soon. Kendrick was waiting for a call. She was supposed to be having dinner with him and his parents tonight. "I need to work on logistics," she said. "I can't just be a no-show at the hospital."

"I'll drop you off at the hotel. You do what you have to do and then call me later and let me know what you've decided."

"I just don't want to drag this out any longer, Tommy."

"And I don't make commitments, and break them. When I promised you I'd stand by you, and love you and protect you, I meant it. So give me a week to honor my vows, and if at the end of the week, you still want out, I'll sign everything, and that's it."

"I'm going to want out, Tommy."

"We'll see. The week hasn't even begun yet."

"Oh? When does it begin?"

"When the competition ends Sunday. I'll be taking the next week off, too, so we can spend the time together."

"Where?"

He opened the truck door for her. "Does it matter?" He smiled at her, a challenge in his piercing blue eyes. "It shouldn't. Not if we're together."

"Tommy, it's not that simple."

"Why not?"

"I—" She broke off, bit her lip. "I need to think about it. I need time."

"You have until this afternoon. Say two? I'll call you after my event."

"I need to go home. I need to sort some things out."

"Talk to Kendrick, you mean?"

She swallowed hard, lifted her chin. "Maybe."

"Sorry, sweetheart. I'm not in a relationship with Kendrick. I'm married to you."

# CHAPTER THREE

BLAKE PACED HER hotel room, fighting panic. Tommy should be finished with his appearance and signing soon. He'd be calling her, wanting her answer, but she couldn't give him one, not yet, not until she'd talked to Kendrick.

She'd tried to phone Kendrick, but he was at the hospital right now, in surgery. He wouldn't be out for another hour, and then he'd check his phone, and maybe she'd hear from him then.

She couldn't leave a 'not making it to dinner with your parents message' on his voice mail. That would be cruel. He was so excited she was finally going to meet them, and looking forward to introducing her to them. He came from a close family. His parents were successful, professionals, pillars of the community. His mom was a pediatric surgeon. His dad was a judge. He'd had a younger sister but she'd died in a car accident with their mom's younger sister, a college grad student, who'd been babysitting Danielle that day.

Blake pressed the bridge of her nose, pained. She should have told Kendrick the truth at Christmas, when he confessed his feelings for her. That would have been the time to tell him. Until then, there had been nothing romantic between them. They'd been friends, good friends, possibly even best friends, but Christmas Eve changed everything when Kendrick said he'd loved her for years, and he couldn't keep it secret any longer. He had to know how she felt.

She'd been caught off guard. She didn't have romantic feelings for him. She didn't think about men—aware that she had one, somewhere, probably across the country, doing his thing, and doing it well. She hadn't expected Tommy to be faithful. It never once crossed her mind that he'd 'wait' for her. He was a rodeo champion, a star. He had legions of women pursuing him. Why he still wanted to be married to her was beyond her.

Her phone rang. She prayed it was Kendrick. Thankfully, it was. "How did surgery go?" she asked.

"Well. A fairly long one. Six and a half hours," he said. "But everything looks good."

"Glad to hear it. You must be tired."

"I could use coffee, or a nap. Or both." He yawned. "So, are you back?"

"No. I'm still here." He didn't respond, and she felt his disappointment. "I'm not going to make it back for dinner," she added quietly. "I'm so sorry. I hate letting you down."

"I don't understand, Blake. Who is this guy? What is he to you?"

She couldn't hide, or deny the reality, not any longer,

not to him. She owed him the truth. "He's my husband."

There. She'd said it. She couldn't take it back.

He said nothing. Just stunned silence. She hated the silence.

"We married three years ago December, in Las Vegas."

"When you were there for Allie's bachelorette party?"

"Yes."

More stunned silence.

"I'm sorry I didn't tell you. I should have told you—" She broke off. "No one knows. You're the first person I've told."

"So, what are you doing there?"

"Trying to get him to sign the petition for divorce. I've been trying for years to get him to sign."

"You didn't have to serve him papers in person. He doesn't have to sign. California is a no-fault state. You could have filed years ago, and had someone serve him with papers."

"I didn't know where he was."

"He's a vagabond?"

"No. He's a—" She bit back the words, torn. She'd kept this secret so long, and it had been a big secret to keep. It felt good to get the truth out in the open, but at the same time, she wanted to protect Tommy. He had a name, a career. There was no reason for him to be part of her and Kendrick's conversation. And once Kendrick had a name, he'd look Tommy up, read about him, come to his own conclusions.

Maybe he'd contact him.

Maybe he'd say something.

She didn't want that.

"I'm going to be taking the week off," she added. "I've been having my headaches and not feeling one hundred percent."

"It's just the medicine."

"I know, but a break would be good."

"If your ex is causing stress—"

"He's not my ex yet."

"He will be, soon, and if he's not making this easy for you, Blake, I can get a lawyer, have him handle this so you're not caught in the middle."

"You're a good friend, Kendrick, and I appreciate your support, but this isn't your fight—"

"I love you, Blake."

She closed her eyes, held her breath and then exhaled. "You know I don't feel that way about you," she said gently.

"Not yet. But you might. Once this guy's out of the picture. Tell me, is he being difficult?"

She pictured Tommy at breakfast, Tommy with his blue eyes and the flash of his straight white teeth when he smiled. And he smiled often. His smile was probably her favorite thing about him. "Not difficult as in threatening, but he doesn't want the divorce. He still believes in us."

"I didn't realize you were a couple."

"We're not. Legally, yes. Emotionally, no."

"When did you last see him?"

"Uh, the weekend we got married."

"He's an idiot then."

She winced. "Don't say that. Tommy's—" She broke off, bit her lip. "Tommy's a really good person. Be mad at me, not him."

"His name is *Tommy*?"

"Don't. Please."

"Are you in love with him?"

"No." *Yes.*

"Then why is this so hard?"

"Kendrick, I need to go."

"When will you be back?"

"Next weekend. Sunday night, probably."

He made a rough sound. "Will you be back?"

"Of course."

But Kendrick didn't say anything and it made her eyes burn. "I'm not disappearing," she said. "I've my residency to finish. My medical exams."

"Where do I fit in?"

"You're still my best friend. That hasn't changed."

"I want more," he said.

She knew he did. But that didn't mean he was right for her. She didn't think anyone was right for her. Not with her health issues. "I'll call you as soon as I'm home."

"I'd feel better if I'd hear from you sooner than that."

"I'll call you in a couple days then."

Even as she hung up, a new call came in with a 406 area code. Montana. Tommy.

Blake sat down in the chair in the corner, and answered. "One week," she said before he could speak. "I need to be home next Sunday. I'm calling in sick for the week, but I must be back at work Monday morning."

"Great. Pack your things. I'm on my way."

"Wait—why?"

"I'm picking you up. You'll stay with me in my rig."

"No. I don't want to stay in the trailer. There's no space. We'd be on top of each other—"

"Now that does sound appealing."

She blushed. "That's not happening."

"I'm just teasing you. But I'd like you closer. The point is spending time together—"

"I told Kendrick about you." That got his attention. Blake took a deep breath, adding, "I told him we're married." Tommy didn't immediately speak. She wondered what he was thinking. "He was surprised." She grimaced. "And not in a good way."

"That would have been uncomfortable."

"I should have told him years ago, but I suppose I thought I'd be able to make it—us—go away, without anyone knowing." She sighed and reached up to pull the elastic from her hair. Just taking out the tight band already made her feel better. "I've promised Kendrick I'll stay in touch with him. That way he won't worry I've been abducted."

SHE'D MANAGED TO convince him not to pick her up, and that she'd just see him at the stadium after he was done competing. She did have studying to do, and she was nervous about seeing him again. Things were happening quickly and she wasn't sure what she was feeling... only that she was feeling. Nerves. Anxiety. Restlessness.

But soon, she reminded herself, this would all be over. One week from now and she'd have the divorce papers signed, and then she'd file the paperwork, and in another six months, she'd be free.

An hour before the rodeo started, Blake showered and dressed, putting on dark jeans and the boots Tommy had bought her in Las Vegas three years ago. She hadn't worn them since and they were stiff, but if she wouldn't wear them tonight, to a rodeo, when would she wear them? She paired the jeans with a white billowy blouse, tucked in at the waist, and a chunky gold and gray bead necklace bought at an artisan market a year ago. With gold hoops in place, she grabbed her suede leather coat and headed to the rodeo.

Tommy found her in the stands before the event started. People clearly knew who he was as he sat down next to her, momentarily filling an empty seat, as she heard the whispers and felt the stares. Tommy seemed oblivious.

"You look gorgeous," he said, smiling at her. He was wearing a long-sleeved lavender-blue shirt tonight, with sponsor logos embroidered on the chest and down the sleeves and, with his black hat and black boots, he looked rugged and sexy.

"Thank you." She wasn't sure where to look because he was smiling at her in a way that gave her butterflies. She didn't want butterflies. She didn't want to feel the pull and attraction. She was getting out at last and, yes, he made her heart do a giddy double beat, but he wasn't right for her, not for long term. Barely for short term.

"There's going to be a dance after tonight's events. Feel like going?" he asked.

She gave him a hard look. "No."

"Then it's just back to my place."

"No. That's not happening, either. We can go have dinner and then I'll return to the hotel, and you return to your trailer and we'll figure out what's what tomorrow, after the finals." A thought crossed her mind. "Where are you competing next week?"

"Austin. Rodeo Austin is a good one."

"But you were just in Houston two weeks ago."

"I never miss Houston. Houston is one of the biggest of them all. The payout this year was over 1.5 million dollars."

"You took some of that home, didn't you?"

"I did well there this year. Houston agrees with me." He looked into her eyes, lips curving ever so slightly. "You've been following me."

"A little," she admitted. "Which is why I'm not sure how Salinas factored into your schedule. It's out of the way, and it's not as much money as some."

"It's an old rodeo, though, and Billy wanted to see some livestock in the Central Valley, so here we are. And here you are."

"I surprised you," she said.

"You did. I used to think you'd show up at the Cow Palace. I'd always look for you there."

"Sorry."

"You're here now," he said.

"For the wrong reasons, I suppose."

"I haven't given up." He reached out, adjusted her hoop earring before returning his hand to his thigh. "You should know that about me. I'm not a quitter."

"You're just fighting for a lost cause."

"My favorite kind," he said, smiling the smile that always made her chest knot and ache. He glanced out to the ring where big tractors were smoothing the dirt-packed arena. "I better go. Don't want to miss my first event." He leaned forward, kissed her brow and rose. "Cheer for me."

"I will."

"Say it with more conviction."

"I always root for you, Tommy. Even if we're not married, I'll still be on your team."

IT WAS EASY to cheer for Tommy, on a Saturday night when the stadium stands were filled, and Tommy, along with the rodeo clown and other competitors, put on a show. Tommy was on fire, earning big points in two of his four events. He and Billy were on top of the leader board with their team roping, and now Tommy had one event left, bull riding.

Blake could see him standing above the chute, checking the ropes, making sure everything was right. Billy was close by, assisting. They looked a lot alike, but it was easy to tell them apart from afar with Tommy's lavender shirt and Billy wearing navy blue. There were others standing around, too, and the man seated next to Blake, explained that one of those hovering was probably the owner of the bull. The livestock were valuable—as important as the cowboys—and received special care.

Then everyone was stepping back and Tommy was on the bull's back. Seconds later the gate opened and the bull shot out, kicking up his back legs, kicking high. The crowd roared approval and it was the longest eight seconds Blake could remember. It was a wild, exciting ride and Tommy nailed it. As soon as the buzzer signaled the eight seconds were over, he launched himself off the bull's back. His fist pumped the air as he ran toward the gate, but suddenly, the bull turned and came charging back. Tommy was fast, and the bull fighters leaped forward to intercept the bull, but the bull wanted Tommy. The bull put his head down and charged Tommy, catching him by the hips, flinging him up, and striking Tommy with his horns as he came down.

Blake had gotten up with the rest of the fans when the

bull caught Tommy, sending him flying, but when Tommy hit the ground and the bull came back for more she covered her mouth, muffling her scream. Thankfully, this time the bull fighters distracted the bull, giving Tommy time to scramble up the side of the arena, climbing out of the ring, but she saw the blood on his face.

Blake didn't know how deep the cut was, but she gathered her coat and purse, and left the stands, heading to the back of the arena where it was blocked off for the organizers, animals, and competitors. A guard stopped her, telling her she couldn't proceed.

Blake squashed her annoyance. "Tommy Wyatt's been hurt," she said.

"Sorry."

"I'm a doctor," she added.

"The PRCA has its own medical team. They're seeing to him now."

The guard's indifference frustrated her. "I'm family," she added.

The guard shrugged. "His brother's back there."

"Yes, but I'm his wife." She could see he didn't know what to think and she added, "You can escort me back to him, if you'd like? He'll confirm who I am."

The guard signaled to someone on the other side of the barricade, and the man in the blue shirt approached. "Says she's Tommy's wife. Want to walk her back to him?"

The man in the blue shirt looked at her, more amused

than surprised. "Tommy's not married, hon."

"Let's go find him. See what he says," she answered tart-ly, not enjoying throwing around her marital status but worried about Tommy.

"I can't take you back. It's not allowed."

"If you get Billy—"

"Hon, it's not going to happen."

"Please don't call me hon." She reached into her purse, pulled out her hospital ID, flashing the badge. "I'm Dr. Blake Eden, and I'd like to be taken to my husband now." She gave him a patient smile, but she wasn't playing. "Ask Tommy if you don't believe me. He'll tell you who I am."

The man in the blue shirt walked her back to the medical tent.

Tommy was being treated on a table at the far end of the tent. He was lying down, holding a cloth to his face, but he turned his head, looked their way as they entered the tent. "I'm fine," he said to Blake. "Just a scratch."

The man in the blue shirt pointed at Blake. "Says she's your missus."

Tommy glanced at her, and then back at the rodeo offi-cial. "She is. Thanks, Scott."

Blake ignored Scott's stunned expression and walked to-ward Tommy where he was being treated by a doctor. "How deep is the laceration?" she asked the doctor.

"Not very deep," Tommy answered, sitting up, reposi-tioning the cloth on his cheek. "I'm good."

"Heading to the hospital to get a CAT scan?" she asked.

"No need." Tommy smiled at her, his laid-back, butter-wouldn't-melt-in-my-mouth smile. "I'm done for the night. I'll just head back to my trailer and get some rest so I can compete tomorrow."

Blake faced the team doctor. "He's not going to the hospital?"

"I can stitch his cheek here—if he wants stitches."

"He doesn't," Tommy said.

She glared at him, disgusted by the pair of them. "I can stitch his cheek, too. That's not the point. His head struck the ground. Hard."

"Tom didn't lose consciousness," the doctor answered. "He's tracking visually. He's not dizzy—"

"Or nauseous," Tommy added helpfully. "No headache."

"Not yet," she said.

"I'll give you two a minute," the doctor said, exiting the tent.

Tommy made a tutting sound. "You scared him away."

"He needs to tell you the truth, not what you want to hear."

"The truth is, I'm done for the night. We can apply liquid stitches to my cheek. I'll be good to go tomorrow."

"You're really not going to go to the hospital," she said.

"I'm really not."

She snorted, exasperated. "Looks like I have to spend the night babysitting you."

"That's not romantic, sweetheart."

"Because it's not romantic. I'm staying with you to make sure you don't have a brain bleed."

An hour later, Blake returned to the stadium parking lot, parked her car in the now nearly empty lot, and threaded her way through the competitors' trailers and trucks, past pens of livestock to Tommy's trailer. She'd checked out of her hotel and brought everything, which wasn't that much as she'd only planned on being here one night.

Tommy was resting when she opened the door to his trailer, his feet up on the small couch, head tipped back, eyes closed.

She stood in the narrow doorway watching him. She felt the same awe she felt the very first time she met him. Felt the same rush of emotion—desire, gratitude, admiration. He was handsome and rugged. Strong. And brave.

Utterly fearless.

# CHAPTER FOUR

*Las Vegas—Three years and three months ago*

TOMMY HAD BEEN around a lot of drunk guys. Rodeos were full of beer and swagger.

It wasn't the cowboys who were doing the hard drinking; it was the spectators who'd come to the show and let their hair down, wanting a good time. Most rodeos sponsored a dance or party during the weekend, where those who weren't ready to go home, could drink, dance, and mingle. Some of the single cowboys would wander in, check out the girls, see if there was anything interesting happening, but Tommy stayed away from those. He wasn't interested in parties where people would get wasted. There were always beautiful women at the dances, beautiful available women, as well as macho guys who thought they could be a professional cowboy, or who'd competed at an amateur level, maybe even briefly at a professional level, and they liked to get scrappy. Alcohol made one scrappy.

The big-name cowboys didn't show up and drink hard. Now in Vegas at the NFRs they might drop by one of the after-parties at one of the sponsor hotels. It was good PR for the Professional Rodeo Cowboy Association and the hotels wanted to see the cowboys and cowgirls there. It made them look good, and Tommy didn't mind meeting up with his brothers and friends for a drink and a little socializing before heading back to his trailer and resting up for the next night's events.

He was on his way to one of the after-parties now, crossing through the noisy hotel casino where music competed with the ringing and clinking of poker machines. He'd almost reached the bar where his brothers were waiting when he saw something that made him pause. A group of guys were following a woman—a very gorgeous woman in a stunning crimson silk mini dress—and she didn't look happy. Tommy stopped walking to watch, wanting to be sure he understood the situation. The men were talking at her, giving her attention she clearly didn't want. She seemed annoyed, as well as uncomfortable, but not fearful.

If one of those guys were her boyfriend, they wouldn't all be chasing her. And if one of those guys had a relationship with her, they wouldn't all be making comments. The comments weren't polite. The comments were pissing him off.

You didn't talk that way to anyone, let alone a single woman walking through a busy, noisy, crowded casino.

He didn't make a conscious decision to intervene. He just did. He intercepted the group as they crossed from carpet to marble floor close to the hotel exit. He stepped between the woman—she was tall, slender, with endless bronzed legs—and the guys.

"Hey, what's going on?" Tommy said, with a friendly smile as he glanced from her, who was even more beautiful up close, to the four guys who were obviously inebriated and definitely obnoxious. "Do we have a problem?"

"Mind your business, cowboy," one of the guys slurred, adjusting his own belt. He had a little silver buckle and was wearing boots. He seemed to think he was tough.

Tommy always thought it was funny when someone called him cowboy. It never made him mad. It just made him smile.

Tommy glanced at the woman in the long-sleeve, short skirt, crimson silk dress, a dress that wrapped her beautifully, dazzled by golden brown curls and stunning gold-green eyes. She was perfection. High cheekbones, delicate chin, full lips, all in a heart-shaped face. She looked like a goddess. It was almost hard to look at her and stare. "Are these your friends?" he asked her.

She shook her head. "No. Most certainly not." Her voice was low, husky, her tone confident. "I've asked them to leave me alone, but they won't."

He turned back to the guys who were bunching up, getting their aggression on. "You heard her, fellows. She's not interested in walking or talking with you. Why don't you move along to the casino, or the bar, and continue having your fun there?"

He didn't wait for a response. He turned, put his out arm out, a barrier between them and her. "Where are you heading?"

She glanced at the guys behind him then looked at Tommy. "I'm trying to get back to my room."

"Are you in this hotel?"

She shook her head. "No I'm two hotels down."

But the hotels in Las Vegas were huge and that could be ten minutes away. "Where are your friends?"

"They're still here celebrating." She glanced again at the guys behind him. "But I'm tired. Ready to call it a night."

"I'll walk you there."

Her sweeping glance took him in from head to toe— black hat, black leather jacket, crisp western shirt, dark fitted denims and boots. "You don't mind?" she asked.

"Not at all." He didn't even look back at the guys, hoping they'd get the hint. Hoping they'd wander back to whatever hole they'd emerged from. But as they walked across the vivid red and purple casino carpet, he could hear the slurred remarks, the complaints, the odd curse. The guys were following. If he were on his own, Tommy wouldn't worry about four against one. The Wyatts had grown up fighting. As the youngest of four tough brothers, he'd been beat up a lot, and eventually, thankfully, learned to hold his own. Turned out Tommy was a natural fighter, too. He didn't mind a blow. He didn't flinch when hit. He happened to be quick, blessed with speed and hard, fast fists.

So no, he wasn't worried about himself. His main concern was keeping her safe.

"I don't know about these clowns," he said. "They seem pretty drunk. They might try something stupid when we step outside."

"They've been stupid ever since they saw me leave the revue."

"Revue?"

She blushed. "One of those male stripper shows."

"I hear they're hot."

She gave him a strange look. "Unfortunately, I picked up my four admirers and haven't been able to shake them since."

"They're just too drunk now. Which means diplomacy will be lost on them. If one of them throws a punch, you need to stay out of the way, because it'll get messy fast."

She looked at him, a dark brown eyebrow arching, her lovely eyes focused on him. "You're not going to try to fight all four?"

"That's the goal. But from the way they're pursuing us, I think it's likely once we leave the hotel, we're going to have a little brawl."

"But not before?"

"Too much hotel security. They'll wait until we're on the street."

She glanced at him again, amusement tinged with curiosity. "You should know I'm not a good fighter."

His lips twitched. "You don't have to be."

"You're comfortable fighting all of them?"

"Hopefully it will not come to that."

"But should it come to that?"

Tommy liked her. She was smart. And beautiful. He didn't think he'd ever felt this way. Just floored. Just looking at her made him feel like a kid. "I should be okay."

"You're not giving me a lot of confidence."

"How about this. I've never lost a fight."

"There are four of them."

"But they're drunk, and stupid." He reached for his phone, quickly tapping out a group text. "I'm letting my brothers know I'm walking you back. That way if I never return, they'll know to come looking for my body."

She shot him a quick, worried glance. "If that's humor, it's not funny."

"It's a little bit funny."

She shook her head. "Maybe I should just alert security. Maybe they can help with the situation."

"They can help with security here on the premises. But they can't help you once you're on the street or crossing the street or walking down the street to your hotel."

"You seem to know a lot about these things."

"I've been coming to Las Vegas since I was seventeen. Kind of my home away from home."

"So they'll do what, when?" she asked.

"They'll make a move when we leave the driveway and

hit the street. And when they do, just step back, let me take care of business. It'll be over soon."

"You're so confident."

He shrugged. "I don't dislike a good fight."

"And the odds?"

He looked at her, winked. "Oh, they're very good."

Everything he'd predicted happened just as he said it would. The guys following them made a move as soon as they were in front of the hotel. The sidewalk was crowded, which was actually in his favor. It wasn't the first time he had to fight four guys at once. It was easier fighting drunk guys than sober, too, and these weren't hardened fighters. The guys had come to Vegas for a good time, and had forgotten what a good time meant, and with too much alcohol in their system, they were hotheaded and irrational.

As each came at him, Tommy needed a couple well-placed punches to knock the guy back or down. Tommy took some hits, but compared to what he experienced in the ring, it was nothing. He had no idea how long the actual fight lasted. It could have been five minutes, could have been fifteen or twenty, but then it was over, and the guys were lying on the ground, groaning, bleeding. One was just out cold. He didn't bother checking on wounds. He didn't care. Instead he turned to her, held an arm out. "Shall we go?"

She nodded.

He stayed close to her side as they left the corner, and the remnants of the brawl.

"You know you're bleeding," she said, holding his arm as they crossed the street.

He dabbed his mouth, and then his cheek. "Not worried."

She looked up into his face, amusement in her beautiful green-gold eyes. "Does anything worry you?"

He had to think a moment before shaking his head. "No." He smiled down at her. "Is that bad?"

He was content seeing her to her door at the Luxor, but she insisted he come into her room so she could examine his cheek, which kept bleeding.

"Facial cuts bleed," he said, brushing off her concern.

"I'm aware of that," she said dryly. "Sit down there, on the edge of the bed. I've got a bandage—"

"I don't need a bandage."

"The Steri-Strip will help. Trust me."

Tommy sat, not because he needed a Steri-Strip, but because she was beyond beautiful. Her skin gleamed, her dress showed off her long legs and sensational figure. He hooked his thumbs over his belt to keep from touching her.

"Are you a Las Vegas fan?" she asked, returning from her bathroom with a tiny first aid kit.

"No. I'm here for work."

She tilted his head to the light, and tearing open an antiseptic wipe, blotted the blood on his cheekbone, and lip. "Based on what you're wearing, are you one of those cowboys here for that big rodeo event?"

"I am."

She opened another wipe and pressed it to his eyebrow. "Are you any good?"

"Not bad."

She squeezed some ointment from a tube and gently spread it over the cuts. "Have you ever won?"

"Yeah."

"You've suddenly gone to one syllable answers."

"I don't want to be a braggart. No one likes those."

She looked down into his eyes, humor in her green-gold irises. "So you're good."

"Mmmm."

"Are you always this charming?"

The corner of his mouth curled. "I am."

She laughed and opened the bandage, carefully pressing the edges of the wound together and then applying the strip to the cut. She added another bandage to the cut above his eyebrow. "You're going to have some significant bruising tomorrow I'm afraid."

"It will not be the first time."

She disappeared, washed her hands, and then returned, drying her hands on a small hotel towel. "You never told me your name."

He stood up, picked up his hat from the bed. "Tommy Wyatt. And yours?"

"Blake Eden."

"That's a beautiful name."

"Don't get sappy on me," she said, beautiful eyes flashing. "It's just a name."

He settled his hat on his head, drawing it low. "You're a little ruthless aren't you, Miss Eden?"

"I am. And not happy that I needed rescuing tonight. I prefer fighting my own battles. It's been a long time since I needed someone to rescue me."

He needed to go, but he didn't want to. "I think you have just rescued me. Saved me a trip to the ER."

"Why do I feel like you would not have gone to the ER?"

"Because nothing was broken—"

"How do you know?"

"I've had enough broken bones to be able to tell."

"And your face?"

"Would have just glued together myself and called it a day." He glanced at his watch. Read a text message. Turned his phone off. "It's late. I'll let you go." He turned at the door. "How long are you in town for?"

"I was supposed to go home Sunday. Thinking of going home earlier. Las Vegas isn't for me."

"It's fun for people looking for a good time."

"That's my problem. I'm never looking for good time."

He laughed. "Why not?"

"I'm your classic A-type personality. I work hard, stress about everything. A perfectionist without a sense of humor."

"That sounds rather dreadful." His gaze skimmed her. "But I don't believe everything you're saying, as you are funny, and you look sensational in that dress. I love the color. It's not really red. It's not orange. It's just… Perfect."

She shook her head, smiled. "You are a charmer."

"I'm a competitor. But I'm honest. I never say something I don't mean."

She looked at him a long moment. "If I wanted to see you again tomorrow, would you have any time? I feel like I owe you breakfast or lunch. Took a little bit of a beating on my behalf tonight."

"And I enjoyed every minute. You owe me nothing. I'm just glad I was there, and was able to help you."

"How about a late breakfast? Eleven o'clock here?"

"Yes."

"That was easy."

He grinned. "What are you implying?"

Her hands went up in mock surrender. "Nothing. But if breakfast isn't good for you—"

"It is. I'll be here."

"Should you need to cancel, just text me."

"Why would I need to cancel?"

"You might be fighting more bad guys."

He laughed, even as his chest filled with warmth. He liked her. A lot. He couldn't even remember when he'd ever been this attracted to anyone. "True. You make good points."

Her lips twitched. "So, should something come up, text me." She rattled off her number.

"Got it," he said.

She arched a delicate eyebrow. "Aren't you going to put it in your phone?"

"I already have it memorized."

Her lips pursed with disapproval. "I don't believe you."

He repeated her number back to her.

"How did you do that?" she asked.

"I'm good with numbers."

"And apparently gifted with an excellent short-term memory."

"I'll be here tomorrow at eleven." He gave her a slow smile. "Looking forward to seeing you, Ms. Eden."

IT HAD BEEN far too easy to fall in love with him.

Blake didn't fall in like easily, never mind love, and Tommy Wyatt was the first person who'd ever made her heart race, and her knees knock. Just looking into his blue, blue eyes, her whole world titled, the axis tipped.

He made her breathless. In his eyes, she saw possibility. Just one look, one smile, and she was hooked.

He was hot, handsome, sexy, strong. He dazzled her. He literally turned her world inside out.

After they'd met for brunch, she spent the spa appointment thinking about him, thinking about when she could see him again, thinking about his invitation to attend the rodeo that night. He told her he'd leave her a ticket at the

Thomas Mack arena. She just had to go to will-call, give her name, and let them know she was on Tommy Wyatt's pass list. She'd asked him if he did this often, give tickets to women, and he'd said no. He said he never did, at least he hadn't in years.

That made her feel good, special, but why did *he* like her? What made her special in his eyes? They were opposites in every way. He was relaxed, funny, physical. She was uptight, driven, intellectual. But he made her laugh, and she loved it. She loved that when he smiled at her, she felt amazing. Warm, happy, safe.

She loved his daring. She loved sitting in the stands that night, watching him compete. She'd never met anyone like him in her life—so strong, so confident, utterly fearless. As he jumped off the bull following the eight-second buzzer, the arena went crazy, cheering for him as if he was a bona fide hero. And maybe he was.

THAT NIGHT THEY couldn't get close enough, couldn't talk enough, couldn't share enough. Even though Tommy had a huge day tomorrow, he didn't want to sleep. He just wanted to learn more about Blake. He loved listening to her talk about her passions and dreams. She was brilliant and passionate, and when she talked about med school, she lit up. Med school was clearly grueling; she was tired, but also elated. It was clear she loved what she was doing, finding it exciting and fulfilling in a way nothing had ever fulfilled her before. She'd been one of the smart girls, but she wasn't as strong in math and science as some of the students she'd gone to college with, and so she made up by working harder. Putting in longer hours.

"I don't mind hard work," she said, nestling in his arms, in his trailer bed. "I was raised with the expectation that I'd always have to work harder than others. In part because I'm a girl, but also because you can't think anything will ever be handed to you. There are no true handouts in life. If you take something for free, it steals a little bit of your self-respect. And so I did what I was raised to do—work hard, keep my head down, focus on my goals, and make no excuses."

She paused, grimacing, wrinkling her nose. "I miss sleep sometimes. I'm always short on sleep, but eventually I'll sleep again, and I'll be in residency somewhere, one step closer to my dream of being a doctor."

"Any idea of what area of medicine you'd like to specialize in?"

She shifted, turning on his chest to look up at him. She lightly touched his jaw, nails scraping the bristles of a day-old beard. "I'm not sure, to be honest. I think it's all interesting. Sometimes, I think being a general practice doctor would suit me best, as I could take care of everyone... families. I'd enjoy the variety, and it'd be wonderful watching children grow up, and being part of a community. But I know insurance companies and medical groups are consolidating practices and being a GP wouldn't be the way it was when I grew up. Successful medicine these days is often focused on quantity of patients one sees, not the quality of medicine provided."

He heard the disgust in her voice and he lifted her hand, kissed it. "That's mostly in cities, I think. Smaller towns still have smaller medical practices."

"But insurance companies are the same whether in big cities or small towns. They're part of the issue. It seems like here in our country, not everyone can afford excellent care, which isn't right if you're seventy and have spent your life paying your taxes and doing your part. Our seniors have helped build this country and I want to be available to them. If I could, I'd make sure every patient of mine was treated like a VIP."

"Why the interest in seniors?"

"I've always been close to my grandparents. I was lucky that both sets of grandparents lived close to us, and we saw a lot of them every week. Both sets would come over on Sunday afternoon for dinner, and my dad and mom would also have them over during the week, whether for a meal or dessert and conversation. After my mom's dad died, my mom's mom moved in with us. She still misses my grandpa. She's not the same."

"No divorces?"

Blake shook her head. "No, none."

He kissed her then, not to silence her, but to savor her, and the emotion. Everything inside of him wanted to protect her, to lift her, support her, to help her achieve her dreams. He'd met a lot of beautiful women in his life, but he'd never met anyone like her, or anyone who mattered so much to him. So what that they'd only known each other two days? She was his. She was meant to be his. He was sure of it in every cell and nerve and bone of his body.

"I think you're amazing," he said later, as she drifted off to sleep in his arms.

She kissed his chest, and then again. "I think you're amazing, too."

He brought her close, holding her securely, staying awake until she slept, and then he made a promise to God. *I will take care of her forever. If she lets me.*

"Let's get married." She clasped his face, his bristled jaw rough against her palms. Blake leaned close, kissed him, once, and again. "I know it sounds crazy, but I don't want to lose you. I can't lose you. I've only just found you."

"You won't lose me. I can promise you that."

"I can lose you tomorrow night, one of your crazy dare-devil events. Something could happen—"

"Nothing is going to happen. I promise you."

"You can't promise me that. You can't make promises like that. It doesn't work."

"I can tell you this; I will never not love you. I know we've only just met, but you're the one I've been waiting for.

You're the one that God made for me."

"No, I think I was supposed to meet you." She smiled faintly, tightly. "I think the whole reason I came on this trip was to meet you. It's not something I normally do and I regretted coming, but then I met you and it's changed everything."

"I think there was a higher power at work," he said.

"So many things had to happen. The universe had to line up—me, leaving the club. The guys following me. You there at the right moment…" She shook her head. "But you were there, and it changed everything."

"Hopefully for the good," he said.

She searched his eyes. "I never want to leave you."

"Then don't."

"That's not possible. I have med school. I have obligations." She paused, smiled. "Come to San Francisco with me."

"And do what?" he asked, twirling a curl around his finger.

"Good question." She snuggled closer. "But I like being with you. I love being with you. You make me feel good and safe. I almost never feel safe."

"Because of guys hassling you?"

"No, not like that, not an external threat. More of an internal thing." She pressed her cheek to his chest and closed her eyes, just wanting to stay there forever. His chest was hard, and his heart beat steadily, and he smelled like everything she'd ever wanted—love, hope, security. Love, good-ness, strength. Love, joy, laughter. "I get anxious sometimes, and I'm afraid I will fail, that I won't be able to be who I want to be, that I won't be able to achieve what I want to achieve. It can be overwhelming, the fear. I still have so many years ahead of me, so many years where I could crash and burn—"

"You won't."

"I might. I've had some close calls. I've had a course I had to repeat. I was the only one that semester who failed it. And the thing is I worked my butt off. I studied and studied and talked to the professor and never missed a class, and I still bombed. It was terrible. I couldn't even imagine what I'd tell my parents if I was put on academic probation. They would have been so disappointed in me."

That night, after the closing ceremonies with all the awards and belt buckles and trophy saddles, Tommy and Blake celebrated his All-Around Cowboy title with his brothers and friends, and then they slipped away, just the two of them, driving to one of the Vegas wedding chapels open twenty-four hours a day, seven days a week. At the chapel, they said their vows and were pronounced man and wife. There were some formalities, paperwork to be signed, and more paperwork to be filed later at the courthouse, but when they returned to Tommy's trailer at two thirty in the morning, they returned happy and married, with their whole lives ahead of them.

Sunday morning everything was already changed.

The NFRs were over. The ten days of competition had ended. Blake's bachelorette weekend had ended, too. The bride had returned to Los Angeles where she was in law school at UCLA. The other girls were on flights, or driving, back to their homes. It was time for Blake to fly back to San Francisco and return to school. But as she kissed Tommy goodbye at the Las Vegas airport, she felt panic. And pain.

When would she see Tommy again?

"I'll be there for Christmas," he promised. "That's just a couple weeks away or, if you'd rather, join me in Montana for Christmas. My family will love you."

Whereas, her family wouldn't love him. Her family wouldn't be okay with what they'd done.

But she pushed that from her mind, not wanting to ruin the goodbye. She'd deal with the fear later. Reality would intrude later. She kissed him as if she'd never see him again, afraid, so afraid.

"Call me when you land," he said, wiping away her tears. She nodded.

"If you need me to come out sooner," he said, "just say the word. I've got a long break coming. I won't compete again until mid-January. All I have is time… time I want to spend with you."

They were boarding her flight now and on the final boarding call. Blake shouldered her carry-on bag, and gave Tommy one last kiss goodbye before heading to the gate agent with her ticket.

It was a short flight home, less than an hour, and she slept, exhausted. Her dad was at the airport to pick her up. He looked somber. "What's wrong?" she asked, climbing into his car at the airport terminal.

"Grandma's not well."

"Oh, no! Why didn't you call me?"

"You deserved a little holiday." But he sounded bleak and Blake knew it was serious. Her dad loved to laugh. He was the ultimate jokester. "Did you have fun?"

"I did."

"Have lots of good girl time?"

She thought of Tommy and the nights in his trailer, and how amazing she'd felt in his arms. "Yes," she said, because now wasn't the time to mention Tommy. She needed to get her parents together. She needed to make sure they were in the right frame of mind.

But a week later, a routine blood test came back, and the results weren't good. They weren't good at all.

Blake couldn't tell Tommy. Or, more correctly, she wouldn't tell him. This was a serious battle, one she'd have to fight on her own. And as the weeks went by and she faced the new year, she realized it wasn't a new year. She wasn't a new person. She couldn't be married to Tommy, either.

Blake couldn't believe what she'd done.

Married? What on earth could she have been thinking?

Clearly, she'd been tired, stressed, living in a fantasy. She had no future with Tommy. She had to stop this. Had to end this. She tried reaching out to him, but he didn't want to hear that it was over. He refused to accept that it was over. He wanted to see her. He wanted to get together and talk everything through, only she couldn't see him, there was no talking everything through. It just had to end. *Now.*

Seeing Tommy would make it impossible to walk away.

Tommy was disruptive. Tommy made her choices impossible. He made her want things and dream about things, dream about a life, she couldn't have. It wasn't fair to him, and it wasn't fair to her. She couldn't explain it to him, either. He just had to accept that she'd lost her head. She'd lost focus. She was in med school. Her parents had invested everything they had for her to attend school. She couldn't blow it. She couldn't handle the stress of breaking anyone's heart, never mind Tommy Wyatt's, but better to end things quickly now, than get so entangled, she'd destroy him later.

Mid-January home, Blake wrote a brief letter, letting Tommy know that she couldn't cope with med school and a relationship. She apologized for disappointing him. She suggested it might be possible to get an annulment. Was the ceremony even valid, if they hadn't gotten a marriage license beforehand? She ended the letter by wishing him well, pleading with him to let her go. She didn't want to see him. She wouldn't speak with him. It had to end and, from her point of view, it was over.

Blake mailed the letter the same day. She considered

changing her phone number, but that was too dramatic. She didn't think he'd reach out, but she didn't want to be tempted, and she refused to feel remorse. She was the wrong person for Tommy. She had issues, serious issues, and she'd never be what he wanted or needed her to be. She'd gotten caught up in a dream. Their days together had been fantasy. But like fantasies it was unrealistic.

Resolved, Blake focused on med school. She focused on moving forward. She focused on her goals. And yes, she would think about him, how did you not think about someone like him? But, ultimately, with time it got easier. She knew from the attention he received at the stadium, beautiful women loved him, they threw themselves at him. He wouldn't be lonely long. He was no longer her responsibility or problem.

Now if only he'd sign the divorce papers. That was the last step, the last task, the last thread binding them together.

# CHAPTER FIVE

I T HAD TAKEN every bit of Blake's courage to come to Salinas yesterday. She'd been panicked, and anxious, but being anxious wouldn't help.

She had to let go of the personal feelings and be professional. Detached. Emotion wouldn't help either of them.

There were things he could do to make the divorce harder, but she prayed if she were good to him now, he'd be sympathetic and good to her in return and just let the past go.

And yet, as he walked toward her, broad shouldered and handsome, her chest ached. He still made her want impossible things.

"Sorry to keep you waiting," he said, small duffel bag in his hands.

"I've been talking to some of the bull fighters. Amazing guys."

"They probably thought the same about you."

She took the duffel from him. "I didn't realize they have to compete to get their jobs. You don't just sign up to be a bull fighter."

"It's not a job most people would be qualified for."

Then he smiled at her, and her breath caught in her throat. Tommy's smiles were the best. There was nothing, and no one, like him.

"So, what are your plans?" he asked.

"I'm going to get my things and return so I can keep watch over you tonight."

"If you're that worried, I can ask Billy to stay with me."

"But I'm here," she answered. "And he might be better looking, but I'm more qualified."

"I'd rather look at you any day."

She smiled, and then he swayed on his feet, and her smile disappeared. "You're not feeling great, are you?"

"I'm fine," he said, but when he did another sway, she went to his side, wrapped an arm around his waist, and held him upright.

"Let's get you to your trailer now, shall we?"

They exited the stadium and started across the huge parking lot. Tommy wasn't fine. He wasn't steady on his feet. His steps were irregular, off-balance, his boots making a hard thudding sound on the asphalt. She was glad when they arrived at his trailer, and even happier when he eased himself down onto the foot of his bed.

She helped take one cowboy boot off, and then the other. He said thanks but his focus was off. He was definitely disoriented. "How are you feeling, champ?" she asked, setting the boots down and sitting next to him on the edge of the bed.

"Fine."

"I don't think that's true." She held up a finger and made him watch her finger as she moved it from right to left. He couldn't follow her finger. "You've got a pretty good knock on your head. You need to heal."

"Sweetheart, we get knocked around all the time. I would go right back out there, injured or not."

"You know all about TBI—"

"Is that like TMI?"

"No. It's traumatic brain injury, and it's not just an injury that you deal with now, it can become post-concussion syndrome, which creates severe problems, ranging from loss of short-term memory, to difficulty performing daily tasks. You don't want to have brain damage."

"I don't, no."

"But repeated concussions can change your future. If you don't take care of yourself, you won't have a future down the road. Studies on PCS have shown an increase in brain disorders, mood disorders, and shorter lifespans. You're too smart to pretend this isn't a problem."

"That's why I wear a helmet now when I ride."

"Haven't you won enough titles? Haven't you won enough money? Or is the issue that you have no other plan? That you're going to ride until you die? Because as I understand it, in your career, it's how it can end."

"You're certainly cheery."

"You're not taking this seriously."

"I won't compete forever. I plan on shifting to something else, but that's not now. I'm at the top of my game. I'm in the best shape I've ever been. I'm riding and roping better than ever, too."

"But what about Bessie the bull tossing you on your head? That's a risk you take every time you ride."

"Bessie the bull is a work hazard. But I know what I'm doing."

"Is that what you were telling yourself when you were sailing over Bessie's horns?"

"To be fair, the bull's name was Vengeance, not Bessie."

She refused to be moved by his smile. She wasn't going to be charmed by the crinkled eyes, the deep dimple in one cheek. This was serious. "It doesn't matter what the bull was called. What matters is that you're being as stubborn as a bull now. You're acting like you can live forever, but we don't get to live forever. And when you have a brain as good as yours, why risk it? Why not walk away while you're doing well? While you're feeling well? While you can walk away?"

"Is this the doctor speaking or the wife speaking?"

She wasn't going to touch that one, either. "It's common sense speaking." She glared at him. "If you compete tomorrow, I'm leaving. I'm not going to stay. I'm not willing to stay and watch you risk further injury, permanent injury. The week is off, too. I'd be done. Done. Done. Done."

He lifted an eyebrow. "You're giving me an ultimatum? My career or you?"

She stepped closer, hands on her hips, chin up so she could look straight into his impossibly blue eyes. "Not giving you an ultimatum, your career or me, I'm giving you an ultimatum about *tomorrow* or me. I'm not going to stick around and watch you ride when you know in your heart you should not be competing. They should be telling you you can't ride. It's insane to me that they let you, the athlete, make the decision. That's not okay. Obviously, athletes are competitive, and you are as competitive as they come, but someone should be telling you this is not okay. I would hope if your mom was here she would be telling you it's not okay."

"You know I come from a long line of rodeo cowboys. It's what we do. It's who we are."

"What if you came from a different family? What if your family expectations had been different? You would probably be a lawyer, or a doctor, or something where you'd be using your brain for good. Not using your brain as a punching bag."

"I can assure you, I try not to use it as a punching bag."

"The night you saved me from those guys in Las Vegas, you took some hard hits."

"And I was fine." He smiled at her, his charming smile. "I didn't suffer any lasting damage."

"But you play with fire, Tommy. It's just a matter of time. You know that, don't you?"

"I had no idea you cared so much."

"I care more than you know." She met his gaze, held it. "But I won't be distracted. You've a concussion. Your head needs a break. Your body needs to heal. Do yourself a favor, do the mature thing. Withdraw from tomorrow."

"I could be taking home big money tomorrow."

"Do you need money that badly?"

"Money's always nice."

"If you're short on funds, I can give you some money. I'll drive to the nearest ATM right now, pull out whatever you need—"

"That's very sweet of you, but I don't want your money."

"Then what do you want?"

"I want a life with you."

"Then it sounds like you made your decision, and since you're not competing tomorrow, why don't we figure out where were going to go in the morning? Because, to be honest, I don't want to hang out here any longer."

"Where do you want to go?"

"I don't know. Except, I don't want to be close to the Bay Area. I don't want to run into someone who knows Kendrick."

"Is Kendrick that well-known?"

She hesitated. "His family is. They donate lots of money and are very involved with philanthropy. Kendrick already sits on lots of boards."

"He's wealthy."

"His family is, but that's not why I care about him. He's

been a really good friend. He helped me a lot through medical school. I got behind, and if he hadn't studied with me, and pushed me, I wouldn't have succeeded."

"How about Montana?"

She blinked, not following the transition. "I've only heard good things about it."

"Why don't we go to Montana? To the ranch. We'd go stay with my family."

Blake had never been to Montana. She couldn't even imagine what the Wyatt ranch would be like. And stay with his family? She wasn't sure about that either. "Can we find a more neutral place?"

"You mean like Vegas?"

"Not Vegas. I haven't been back there since we, uh, met."

"So, what would you suggest?"

"Maybe just a small town somewhere? Or maybe to Southern California… we could go to Laguna or somewhere near the beach?"

"Why the beach?"

"Why not? It'd be warm and relaxing. We also wouldn't know anyone." She hesitated. "I worry that being at your place will not be comfortable for either of us."

"I don't think you'll find it uncomfortable at the ranch. It's just my granddad, my mom… and, yes, Sophie and Joe are on the property, but they have their own house and lots of little people keeping them busy."

"But what would you tell them? How would you introduce me? Hey all, here's my wife, thought I'd bring her home and show her around."

"We don't really say hey all, or ya'll in Montana. But if you'd like me to introduce you as my wife—"

"*No.*" She frowned. "I most definitely don't think we should do that. No one should know we're married." She paused, realizing she didn't know if he'd ever told anyone in his family. "Does your family know? Did you tell them?"

"No."

Relief rushed through her. "So, what would you tell them about me? If I were to go there for a week how would you introduce me?"

"I'll introduce you as Dr. Blake Eden, a woman I care for."

Heat washed through her, making her tingle. "And when I disappear and they never see me again?"

He shrugged. "I'll tell them it didn't work out. Things happen. They know that."

She thought about it for a moment, and then another moment. No one would know her in Montana. She'd see a different part of the country, and not that she believed there was a future with Tommy, but she was curious about his mom. She'd raised four sons on her own. She had to be a strong woman. "I'd like to see where you're from."

"It's an eighteen-hour drive without roadwork and delays. If I was on my own, I might drive all the way through—"

"But you're not on your own, and I'm going to do the driving."

He laughed. "You're going to pull the trailer?"

"Your truck is an automatic, isn't it?" She held his gaze. "I'm serious. Once we're on the freeway, it's just follow the signs and drive."

"Have you ever driven twelve hours a day, never mind eighteen?"

"No. But if I can do eight, I can do twelve. Let's not worry about eighteen. Where would twelve hours get us?"

"Salt Lake City."

"Let's do that, then."

"You'll be miserable."

"You have a bathroom in your trailer."

"I do."

"And a kitchen."

"Yes."

She shrugged. "We'll just stop now and then so I can stretch my legs, use the bathroom, make a snack. We'll be fine." She looked at him expectantly. "When do we leave?"

"We don't," he said. "We can't. I love your enthusiasm, but the trailer is hard to control on mountain passes, even without wind, and there will be significant gusts. With the horses—" He shook his head. "No. No way."

She gave him a long displeased look before walking out of the trailer and going in search of Billy. Billy's trailer was parked next to Tommy's and he was with his horses, grooming them and giving them attention.

"Do you have a minute?" she asked him.

"I have all the time in the world," he answered, offering her a brush so she could help him.

Blake took the brush and gingerly brushed the horse's flank. She wasn't afraid of horses per se, but she'd never been close to them, and these were big. "Has Tommy talked to you about tomorrow?" she asked, while trying to copy Billy's actions.

"No." Billy looked at her. "Why?"

"He shouldn't compete. He has a concussion." She paused. "Anyway, he's told me he won't and he doesn't want to hang out here. But he can't drive right now. He shouldn't drive, and he won't let me drive."

"Go to Carmel or Monterey. He could rest there for a few days."

She gave the horse another slow firm brush, using the time to formulate her thoughts. "We were talking about going to Montana." She tried to keep her voice even. Casual. She really didn't know how much Billy knew about her. "I've never been there, and since he can't compete, he was saying he'd like to go home. See your mom." She paused, looked up at him. "But if he can't drive, and he won't let me drive, I'm not sure how to make this happen. Wasn't sure if you had any bright ideas. I'm worried about him. Concussions damage the brain long term. The brain is everything."

"Tommy has a good brain," Billy agreed.

"So you'll help me find a way to keep him safe this week? He needs the week off. A week where he can just rest."

"I agree. Leave this to me. I'll see what I can do."

BLAKE WENT IN search of dinner, bringing food back for her and Tommy. They'd just finished eating and were sitting on the trailer couch watching the news when a knock sounded on the trailer door.

"It's open," Tommy called.

Billy entered. "Everyone decent?"

"Unfortunately," Tommy answered.

Blake lightly elbowed him in the side, before smiling up at Billy. "Hi."

"I have good news," Billy said, leaning against the small dining table. "Joe and Sophie are going to drive your truck and rig home. They were coming this way anyway. It's Sophie's parents' anniversary. So, they'll fly in, pick up your rig, visit her folks, and then drive home."

"That's ridiculous." Tommy rose but then wobbled a bit on his feet. He put a hand out to brace himself.

"You're not steady, Tommy," Billy said. "Let Joe play the big brother and get your trailer and horses home. It makes him feel useful."

"It's a long drive, and a hassle—"

"Sophie is looking forward to the break from the kids. She hasn't been home in almost two years."

"But the horses," Tommy protested.

"Will be in great hands. Sophie's parents live in the country. They have a dairy farm with lots of land, so Joe will be able to exercise the horses without inconveniencing anyone."

Billy looked at Tommy. "Bottom line, it's settled."

"So, what am I supposed to do?"

"Whatever you want to do. Fly home. Take a train. Hike."

"Very funny."

Billy glanced at Blake, smiled. "He's all yours."

She smiled at Tommy's brother because he had the Wyatt charm in spades. "Lucky me."

Billy laughed. "Since we've got that handled, I'm going to call it a night. You guys take off whenever you're ready tomorrow. Just leave the keys with me. Joe and Sophie will be here around noon. They're arriving in time to watch the finals, and then tomorrow night will head on to Tulare."

"I ought to be in those finals." Tommy didn't look happy.

"But you're not, and thanks to you dropping out, I've improved my odds considerably."

"I should get a percentage of your earnings."

"Yeah, that's not happening." Billy opened the door, smiled. "Good night."

THEY LEFT EARLY Sunday morning to make the nonstop flight out of San Francisco into Bozeman, Montana. Blake drove them to the city, and they stopped by her apartment briefly so she could pack for Montana since Tommy said it'd be cold and windy, but then, it could also be sunny, possibly snow, or not.

Not helpful, she thought, facing her closet. Aware that she didn't have much time, Blake grabbed her heaviest coat, warm fleece lined boots, running shoes, sweats, sweaters, pajamas, and a few more tops and jeans. She'd never been on a ranch before, but she'd seen plenty of TV shows featuring ranches. She couldn't imagine needing anything very fancy, and so she left all of her good clothes and jewelry home.

The flight to Bozeman was short, just two hours, but because of the time change they arrived at eleven thirty and Tommy's grandfather came to pick them up. Blake could tell that Tommy was glad to see his grandfather, having told her before that his grandfather, Melvin, had raised him after his father died. Tommy had no recollection of his own dad, who died when Tommy was just two.

His granddad gave him a quick hard hug, and then stepped back to be introduced to Blake.

"Granddad, this is my girlfriend, Dr. Blake Eden. I invited her home this week. Thought I'd show her a little bit of Marietta, Montana."

Melvin Wyatt took Blake's hand, and then leaned down and gave her a kiss on the cheek. "Welcome to Montana. If

Tommy gives you a hard time, you let me know. I'll be sure to straighten him out."

Blake smiled, already charmed by the gruff old man with the white handlebar moustache. "There's no need for that," she said. "Tom is a gentleman."

"So, what kind of medicine do you practice?" Melvin asked, as they claimed their luggage from the baggage carousel.

"I'm interested in general practice. I like treating everyone—the whole family. I'm just finishing my residency now and will start interviewing for positions in the coming months."

"We could use a good GP here," Melvin said. He tried to take one of the bags from Tommy but Tommy wasn't having any of it. "Marietta's just lost Dr. Giddings. He'd been here forever—ever since Tommy's dad was a baby. He would have stayed practicing too, but he couldn't see very well. It's a shame. I trusted him."

"We all trusted him. He was my doctor growing up," Tommy said, balancing four bags, his two duffels on top of her roller bag, plus a backpack hanging from one shoulder. "But remember how he always got my name wrong? Every single time. Took me years to realize it was his running joke. Joe was Sam or Billy. Sam was Joe. Billy was Tommy. I was any of the three. Used to tick me off that my own doctor didn't know my name, and then one day I saw him smile, and I realized it was all deliberate, and I never minded the teasing after that."

"He had a good practice." Granddad gestured to the vintage dark blue-green truck in the short-term parking lot across the street. "Just over there."

"You brought the Beast," Tommy said, nodding at the lifted four-door truck with huge snow tires. "Has it snowed lately?"

Melvin shook his head. "It's been warm the last couple of weeks, really warm, but a storm might be moving in later this week. It could also blow right past us. Hard to say. I just thought I needed to get the Harvester out for a drive. It's been a while."

Tommy glanced at Blake. "Granddad is a car aficionado. He used to store them at a warehouse but recently moved them up to one of the barns."

"I'm starting to get rid of them. It's hard to do," Melvin added. "But like Dr. Giddings, I'm getting older, not younger. It's time to make changes."

"This is the one I want," Tommy said. "It's a 1967 International Harvester four-by-four. Granddad is only the second owner. Granddad, you bought it when it had, what? Thirty thousand miles?"

"About that," Melvin agreed, as they crossed the road to the parking lot. "It's over two hundred thousand now. Hard to find parts so I baby it." He looked at Blake. "Did you come prepared for snow?"

"I brought some of my winter clothes," she said. "Do

you really think it'll snow? I haven't seen snow in years."

"You never know here. During spring we can have four seasons in one day." Melvin stopped next to his big vintage truck. "Where's home?"

Blake had never seen a truck like this one. But then, her dad wasn't a car guy, and she certainly had never paid attention to cars before. "I'm from San Francisco. For snow, folks head up to Lake Tahoe, but my family never did that. We weren't a ski family."

"Tommy's mom grew up not far from Tahoe," Melvin answered. "Little town called Grass Valley. Heard of it?"

"I have. But I haven't been there. I haven't traveled as much as I would have liked."

"Too busy going to school," Melvin guessed, helping Tommy stow the suitcases in the back of the lifted truck.

"Pretty much," she agreed, thinking of the past decade devoted to school and medicine. "I'm ready for a little vacation, though. Looking forward to seeing the ranch."

Tommy took the keys from his grandfather. Melvin didn't complain. He was about to open the passenger door in the back when Blake stopped him. "If that's for me, thank you. But if you're planning on riding back here—please don't. I'm quite happy to be in the back."

"You've just arrived," Melvin answered. "You'll want the better view."

"I can see out the window just fine," she answered, slipping under his arm and climbing into the back. "Besides, I'm smaller than you. My legs are shorter. And then there's seniority," she added, smiling.

Granddad Wyatt frowned. "You're our guest."

"My dad would be horrified if I allowed you to sit in the back. Please, I'm happy sitting back here. I promise." She gave him her warmest smile. "This way you two can catch up, and I can relax. I'm a bit of a nervous flyer, so I'll just take some deep breaths and calm down."

Tommy had taken the driver's seat but he turned then to look at her. "I didn't know you were a nervous flyer."

"It's not something I like to advertise."

"I could have held your hand," Tommy said.

"You didn't hold her hand?" Melvin asked Tommy as he settled into the front passenger seat. "I'm sure it was a bumpy flight. It always is over the mountains."

Blake blushed. "I'm good. Really." And she was. She felt surprisingly happy being in Montana, strangely free. She was glad to have a break from her world in San Francisco. She'd left messages with everyone at the hospital, and had received clearance from her supervisors, so for the next week, she could relax.

Her gaze shifted to the front, to the width of his shoulders, and the bare nape of his neck which was tan, almost sunburnt. It was obvious he spent a lot of time outdoors.

He'd been handsome three years ago, but he'd filled out since then, carried a little more muscle, his face had become more defined. He'd settled. Become even more of a man. An imposing man, which made her wonder if *she* could relax with Tommy.

But Melvin was still grumbling. "I just don't know why you'd have a beautiful girl like that, Tom, and not hold her hand. Not sure you have your head screwed on straight."

Tommy looked up, caught her gaze in the rearview mirror and gave her a long intense look, and just that made shivers race up and down her spine.

He was trouble. But then, he'd always been trouble.

# CHAPTER SIX

G RANDDAD SHOT HIM a look. "She's definitely in fine form," he said.

"Good or bad way?" Tommy asked, trying to clarify.

"Good way. She's missed you. Looking forward to having you home," his grandfather answered. "And then there's the fact that you've never brought anyone home before."

Tommy glanced up into the rearview mirror; his gaze met Blake's. Blake didn't have to say anything. He knew what she was thinking. His mom would be disappointed when it ended. Everyone was getting dragged into something they didn't need to get dragged into. Tommy understood this, but he was playing the long game, betting on his odds. Odds, he thought were pretty good. But then, he always believed in himself. You accomplished nothing if you didn't have faith in yourself. Even more importantly, you accomplished nothing if you didn't have faith period.

Thirty-five minutes later, they were nearing the entrance to the Wyatt ranch. Their land stretched in every direction but there was only one way in and out, and it was the main drive.

Granddad's truck wasn't quiet and his mom appeared on the front porch as he parked. He was glad to see her using her walker. She'd been alone at the house while his grandfather picked them up in Bozeman. They didn't like leaving her, in case she fell, but she seemed safe and sound, as well as in good spirits as she lifted a hand, waved.

He smiled, thinking she looked good. She was wearing her favorite blue cardigan with a long gray narrow skirt. The cardigan had pink rose buds embroidered on the right, just below her shoulder. She'd cut her long hair since he'd last seen her, the faded blonde-gray strands cut in a stylish bob, making her look younger.

She'd made an effort to look nice. She didn't wear skirts very often anymore, so she was trying to make a good impression. Tommy hoped the visit would go well. His mom wouldn't be rude to Blake but she didn't always warm up right away. She needed time to get to know people, and sometimes when she hurt, she could be brusque. He hadn't shared any of this to Blake, not wanting to make her anxious. He was just hopeful it would be an easy visit; that Blake and his mom would get along. He had no intention of losing Blake, but at the same time, if his mom took a disliking to Blake, it would make things harder. Significantly harder.

"Mom moves a bit slowly," Tommy said, turning off the truck ignition. "She has rheumatoid arthritis. She's often in pain but it's been better this year since she got on new medicine. But she won't talk about it. She doesn't like to talk about herself, either."

"Summer's a good woman," Melvin said firmly, glancing at Blake over his broad shoulder. He had the same big build as Tommy. If Tommy aged the way Melvin had, he'd be a good-looking older man. "You two will get along fine. Just be yourself, Blake. You'll have nothing to worry about."

Tommy saw Blake look at him again in the rearview mirror before he stepped out of the truck. She was looking a little less confident, but he knew she'd be fine. She could hold her own.

The dogs bounded toward him as he walked around to open the door for Blake. He pet them both, but once he gave a command, they sat, tails wagging, ears alert.

"They won't bite," Tommy said, taking Blake's hand, and assisting her out of the lifted truck. "They sound scary but they're big babies."

"Good to know. I like dogs." She smiled at him and then taking a step from the truck, held a hand out so the dogs could smell her. They immediately pushed their heads into her hand, wanting affection.

"Oh, sweet girls," she said, petting each dog with a different hand, before glancing up at Tommy. "Are they girls?"

"One girl, one boy. I'll get the bags later. Let's get you in the house so Mom can sit down."

Daffodils and crocuses bloomed in front of the house. The front door had recently been painted a dark green. Tommy climbed the steps quickly, and gave his mom a long, warm hug, careful with his hug, though, not wanting to bruise her. "I love your new hairstyle," he said, when he drew back. "You look like a twenty-year-old starlet, Mom."

"Ha!" She batted away the compliment but her cheeks pinkened and her hazel eyes brightened. "You're buttering me up, wanting me to make your favorite banana cream pie."

"I can only hope," he teased.

She gave him another impatient gesture, but it was clear she adored his attention. "Now let's not be rude. Please introduce me to your friend."

Tommy kept a hand on his mom's frail back. "Mom, this is Dr. Blake Eden, my... friend. Blake, this is my mom, Summer Wyatt."

Blake clasped his mom's hand gently. "So nice to meet you," Blake said warmly, giving his mom a real smile, the smile that always knocked him on his butt.

He didn't know what it was about Blake, but she was the real deal. She was everything he'd ever wanted in a woman. Smart, ambitious, successful, caring.

And beautiful. So very beautiful with her golden-green eyes and gold tipped curls. And that mouth... a mouth made for kissing.

Just looking at her made his chest tighten.

Things were either going to go his way in the next six days, or he'd put her on a plane and that would be it.

The interior of the old house was cool and dark. Tommy quickly retrieved the bags while Melvin assisted Summer to the dining room where Summer had set the long table for lunches.

After washing up, Blake and Tommy joined Melvin and Summer at the table. "You made my favorite, Mom," Tommy said, holding Blake's chair before sitting down in his own. "You spoil me."

"It's good to have you home," Summer said, her hand shaking as she reached for her glass of iced tea. "Would you rather have water?" she asked, looking from Tommy to Blake.

"No, this is lovely," Blake said.

His granddad said a blessing and then they focused on eating. Tommy hadn't been exaggerating. His mom had made his favorite lunch, chicken salad sandwiches on a local honey wheat bread that was studded with raisins and dates. The thick sliced bread complemented the savory chicken perfectly. "Mom, while I'm here," he said, after finishing the first half of his sandwich, "what can I do to help you? I'm sure you have a to-do list somewhere."

"Just help your granddad," she answered. "He has a lot on his shoulders with Joe gone."

"Sam hasn't been by?" Tommy asked, surprised.

"He comes by," Melvin said. "But he has his own place, and Joe will be back soon. I'm fine."

"Your granddad should not be doing it all on his own," Summer said sharply.

Tommy saw Blake's head lift, her expression somewhat

startled. At least his mom wasn't being short with her. "Granddad won't have to do anything on his own, not with me here."

"Hope you'll be able to entertain yourself while Tommy's working the ranch," Summer added, looking at Blake.

Blake smiled at her. "I've brought my laptop and have a lot of work I can do."

"Blake's studying for her medical boards," Tommy explained. "She also has work she has to do as part of her residency. She'll love having me busy each morning."

Summer kept her focus on Blake. "What area of medicine?"

"General practice. I want to be able to take care of the whole family. It's my goal."

"I was telling Tommy that our family doctor, Dr. Giddings, was retiring soon."

Summer shook her head. "I liked him better than the doctor I'm seeing now. Don't know why I had to change."

"You can still see Dr. Giddings, Mom," Tommy said. "But you needed to see a specialist for your arthritis. Dr. Giddings wasn't doing enough to manage it. You needed better care—"

"Hmph," Summer sniffed. "Dr. Freckles is a lot more money and is not very pleasant."

Tommy grinned. He glanced at Blake. "His name isn't Dr. Freckles. It's Dr. Winkler and he has freckles." He tried to be stern with his mom. "You can't call him that, Mom.

It's not nice."

"He's not nice."

Tommy began gathering the lunch plates. "Granddad, I'll just clear the table and then meet you outside? What will we do first?"

"You okay to ride?" Melvin asked.

"I am." Tommy glanced at Blake, eyebrows raised. "Nothing fancy, Doc. Just your basic trail riding."

"That's a fact," Melvin added. "I'm too old for the fancy stuff."

BLAKE FOLLOWED TOMMY upstairs. He was carrying their bags and explaining to her where everything was. "This is my room," he said, pointing to a room at the end of the hall. "I used to share it with Billy, but when he comes home, he, Erika and the baby, stay over at Joe's. We passed their house on the way in. It was that new log cabin just before ours."

"I wondered," she said. "That's nice that Joe and Sophie aren't far."

"Sophie is amazing with Mom. She's also managing Joe quite well." Tommy flashed a smile as he opened a door, revealing a bathroom, and then continued to a room in the middle of the hall. "This is Sam's room, and you can stay here, or you can have Joe's old room."

"Doesn't matter," she answered.

"Then let's put you in Sam's room," Tommy answered.

"You're closer to me that way."

He opened the door, placed the luggage on the floor. It wasn't very big bedroom, but it had a lovely antique bed frame, a blue duvet cover, and a thick blue and green block quilt folded at the foot of the bed. There was also a big dresser, and medals, ribbons, and belt buckles hanging on one wall. There were also shelves filled with more awards. "Is your room like this, too?" she asked, gesturing to the trophies.

He smiled ruefully. "Time to take them down?"

"No. It's impressive."

"Mom likes to keep our rooms the way they were when we were young."

"My mom is the same," she assured him, and she thought it was sweet. These big tough cowboys coming home to childhood bedrooms. They loved their mom, they loved their grandfather, and they loved God. You couldn't get much more wholesome than that.

"I'm going to change and head out with Granddad," Tommy said. "But if you need anything, tea, water, snacks, feel free to help yourself in the kitchen. Teas are in the upper narrow cabinet near the stove. Mom usually has some cookies in the cookie jars. They'll probably be shortbread or a ginger crisp since I'm here—"

"She made your favorite cookie?"

"Always. And if it was Billy here, it would be peanut butter—chewy. For Sam it's chocolate chip—slightly burnt. Joe is oatmeal raisin."

"You have a good mom."

"Yes." He stood in the doorway, filling it almost completely. "Not that we're messing around, but Mom has a strict rule. No sex before marriage, not in her house."

"And we're not telling her we're married," she said.

"Not telling anyone," he agreed before lowering his voice and giving her a long, slow once-over. "But, should you, my gorgeous girl, feel like sneaking into my room late at night, I won't tell anyone that, either."

A shiver of anticipation raced through her, anticipation she shouldn't feel as nothing was going to happen this week. But when Tommy looked at her, she couldn't focus on anything but him.

She didn't want anything, or anyone, but him.

They were opposites in every way, and yet, somehow, the fact that they were so very different worked. It was part of the energy, part of the attraction. Guys in med school didn't look like Tommy. Doctors didn't look like Tommy. Not even the handsome ones.

Kendrick was handsome, but he didn't give her butterflies, or make her feel tingly on the inside. Tommy didn't have to touch her for her to melt. Just a glance from those blue eyes and she went hot and cold, and light-headed.

It was hard to remember to breathe around Tommy. Hard to remember anything.

She changed from her travel clothes into jeans and a T-shirt and sweater and headed outside, finding a spot of sunshine just outside the barn where she could watch Tommy and his grandfather inside saddle horses.

She was too far away to hear them, but Melvin said something to Tommy and Tommy looked up and smiled at his grandfather. It wasn't a fake smile, or patronizing. It was a smile that was open and loving. A smile of love.

It struck her that Tommy smiled at her the very same way. He smiled at her as if she were the best thing he'd ever seen. It was crazy to have someone smile at you like that, to have someone look at you the way Tommy looked at those he loved. With tenderness, and pride, and protective pleasure. Life was so short and yet he made even the smallest of moments feel big, and special. Like saddling a horse with his grandfather.

Tommy knew how to live. He knew how to be present. Maybe that was part of her attraction to him—he was so fully alive. He radiated strength and conviction, warmth, and energy. She loved his energy… that vitality.

If she didn't need to be close to hospitals, she could see herself here, in his world. She could love these people of his. It would be easy to take a job in a small town and come home to Tommy every night.

Although to be fair, he had to be at home. Right now, he was still on the road, competing. He was only ever not competing for the month between mid-December to mid-January. That was his only real break, and it wasn't enough. She couldn't follow him on the road, and so few of his big events were near her.

It was so confusing, these thoughts and feelings.

Being here, she didn't feel as if they were done. Being here, she felt as if they were just beginning. But was that realistic?

She'd married him because she loved him. It was the one thing she had done for herself. It had been impulsive, yes, and selfish, but it had also been an act of defiance against fear, and limitations, and the future unknown. She'd given him her heart and she'd never taken it back.

He still had her heart.

She still loved him, and only him.

Blake didn't want to be his ex-wife. She didn't want to divorce Tommy. But how could they stay married if they if they always lived apart?

AFTER DINNER, TOMMY and Blake had done the dishes and then Blake had gone upstairs to study, while Tommy spent some time with his mom and grandfather watching the news and talking about things happening in the area, as well as within the family. Tommy hadn't been home since Christmas so there was a lot to catch up on.

Tommy helped his mom up to bed, and then went by Blake's room to say good night. But just before he knocked on her closed door, he heard her voice, and it made him pause.

She was talking to someone, and it sounded an awful lot like she was talking to Kendrick from the way the conversation was going.

Tommy didn't want to eavesdrop, but he wasn't thrilled that Blake was having to be so defensive. He considered walking away, and then he decided maybe he wouldn't. He rapped firmly on the door, and then announced himself. "It's me," he said, opening the door, discovering her seated cross-legged in the middle of the bed.

She gave him a frazzled look, but he didn't offer to leave. Instead, he closed the door behind him and took the old rocking chair in the corner. The rocking chair had been made by his great-grandfather, who'd been a master craftsman in the old country before emigrating to America.

He stretched his legs out and gently rocked as Blake wrapped up her call. When she hung up she gave him a haunted look. "I've been so stupid."

"What's wrong?"

"That was Kendrick. He's quite upset I'm here in Montana with you."

"Why?"

She shrugged. "He didn't expect me to go on a trip with you."

"Had you promised to marry him? Have you confessed your love for him?" he asked.

"No." She drew her knees up to her chest and wrapped her arms around them. "But he cares for me and he's worried he's losing me."

Tommy didn't want to celebrate another person's pain, but at the same time, she was his first, and he wasn't prepared to lose her, either. "He's welcome to come out here. We have plenty of room."

"Tommy."

"I'm serious. I'd like to meet the man that has captured your heart—"

"He *hasn't*." She reached up and pushed gold streaked curls back from her forehead. Tears shone in her eyes. "But he's important to me, and he's taken such good care of me, and it's hard to hurt him."

"You're going back to him at the end of the week."

She said nothing, just looked away.

"Well?" he persisted. "Aren't you?"

"It's more complicated than that."

He was getting annoyed, and he didn't want to feel annoyed, not with her, but Kendrick wasn't his problem. "Explain it to me."

"He's a strong Christian."

"Okay."

"He finds this uncomfortable."

"How does he think I feel? My wife's here but thinking about another man—"

"I'm not having an affair!"

"No, but you have someone else waiting for you to be free. I have no one waiting for me, because I didn't let another woman get close to me. I kept those boundaries. I honored our vows—"

"I did, too. I haven't kissed another man. I haven't flirted with another man. I haven't betrayed you in any way, even though I haven't seen you in over three years." She left the bed and paced the room, coming to stop in front of him. "You might have kept your vows, too, but you're no angel. You have hundreds of women worshipping you from afar. They line up at your events and appearances to get you to sign something, maybe their chest, and take photos with you. They stare at you as if you're godlike. While I'm on the other side of the country just trying to survive. It's not easy for me. Falling in love with you changed everything. Loving Tommy Wyatt is like loving a moving target. You're never home. You're never in one place. Your world is danger and risk and pain. It's not a normal world, Tommy. It's not my world."

"Girls might line up, but there is no one else for me. Just you."

"That doesn't change the fact that you're in a different city every weekend. That you're smiling and taking pictures with different women every weekend—"

"I also take pictures with old ladies and babies."

"That's not the point! The point is you belong to every-one... *everyone*... but me."

Tommy was usually quick, but he was only realizing now what she was actually upset about. Blake was jealous. But the fans were just fans. They were part of the career, and while he had obligations to his sponsors, he wasn't into the buckle bunnies or groupies. He wasn't a player, and he'd never chased chicks. He never had. "I only belong to you," he said. "Not my family. Not the PRCA. No one but you."

She stood in front of him, hands in fists. "And yet I can't travel with you." Her eyes shone with tears. "I can't go meet you on weekends. I can't be in the stands to cheer you on, or make sure you're okay after a hard ride. I can't fix your cuts, or tell you not to ride because your head needs to heal." She drew a deep breath. "That's what a wife wants to do. That's what a wife needs to do, but my job traps me in one place, and doesn't give me a lot of freedom. My job means I take care of other people, not you."

"And you don't like that."

She swiped at a tear as it fell. "I *hate* it."

He pulled her down onto his lap. He could feel her resist, but as she settled on his lap, she then sank against him, absorbing his warmth.

"This is bad," she whispered as his arm wrapped around her waist.

"Why?"

"If I get close to you, and enjoy being close, it's going to hurt more when I leave." She drew a shuddering breath. "You know I have to leave."

"Temporarily." He rubbed her back, feeling the lean muscle and the dip of her spine. "It doesn't have to be forever. We could find a way to make it work. I believe that."

"But, Tommy, I don't plan on moving, which means, you'd have to move, but that's not fair to you, and let's be honest, it's not a good option for you, not with your family all here in Montana." She turned to look at him, and her beautiful eyes looked like precious jewels. "I'd hate myself if you moved for me. I already hate myself for being unable to move for you."

"Don't hate yourself. I understand your priorities, and I respect them. I've never imagined you'd drop everything and join me on the road." He kissed her temple. She smelled of vanilla and citrus, lemon blossoms, and something else, something with a hint of spice. "We've never talked about logistics, but maybe it's time we did, and not tonight, when we're tired. We have time. We can play with different ideas; see what we come up with."

"You're making this hard again," she said. "I'm here to get your signature on those papers, not work out living arrangements."

"I know that's your goal. I have a different goal. We can both have dreams."

She lightly elbowed him. "That's not funny. I like you, Tommy. I don't want this to get harder than it already is."

"Good-byes aren't happening for days, so let's just explore our options. There's no real harm in that."

"Unless I'm giving you unrealistic expectations?"

He laughed softly and dropped a kiss on the top of her head. "You're not."

She settled against him, her body curving into his. "I don't hate you, Tommy."

"I know you don't, sweetheart." He wrapped his arms around her and just held her. She slowly relaxed, her breathing becoming more even. They didn't speak. They just sat there in the rocking chair, and he rocked her, aware of her fatigue. His Blake, with all her brilliant mind and lovely lines and limbs, wasn't getting the rest she needed.

Just one more reason she needed him in her life.

And one more reason why he wasn't going anywhere.

BLAKE WOKE AT midnight, and stretched, realizing she was still in her jeans and T-shirt. She'd been put to bed dressed.

It took her a moment to remember she'd been sitting on Tommy's lap, and he must have rocked her to sleep.

And then tucked her into bed.

She lifted her hips, unsnapped and unzipped her jeans, and tugged them off, and then unhooked her bra from beneath her shirt, and pulled that off, too, taking the strap down one arm, and then the other, and then she lay back down and curled up and thought of him.

Holding her.

Kissing the top of her head.

Making her feel safe.

If Tommy were a superhero, that would be his power. Making her safe. No one else had ever made her so secure.

Or happy.

But happiness seemed almost like a weakness. Was she entitled to happiness? Was anyone?

Certainly, her parents wouldn't begrudge her happiness, but if her happiness meant leaving them? There were no other children. She was it. And they'd nearly lost her twice already. They'd fought with her to keep her on earth.

Was that how she repaid her gratitude? By moving away?

And then when everything went south again, would they blame themselves for letting her go? For not being vigilant?

Blake lived with guilt. It haunted her. The more others did for her, the heavier the guilt became.

This was why she needed medicine. She had to give back. She had to become a giver, not a taker. She had to infuse her life with meaning. Surviving another five years wasn't the goal. It wasn't what drove her. What drove her was helping others, the way she'd been helped, supported, healed.

To be a healer… that was the ultimate. It was everything.

But as she lay there in Tommy's brother's bedroom, it was hard to believe that Tommy wasn't worth the fight.

Hard to believe he wasn't everything. But if she loved him, if she gave in to the love, his world would change.

And she didn't want that. Not now, not ever.

# Chapter Seven

B LAKE WAS NORMALLY an early riser, but the curtains in her room were heavy and lined with a black-out liner so that it was quite late when she finally got out of bed. The kitchen was empty, but the coffeepot was hot and full. She looked around and found a cup, poured coffee, and then sat down at the round kitchen table trying to wake up.

Blake heard Mrs. Wyatt's walker coming down the hall and she sat taller. Summer Wyatt entered the kitchen in gray knit trousers with a matching zipper jacket.

"Good morning," Blake said, rising.

Summer paused, gestured for her to sit back down. "I'm not the queen, but thank you, that's very polite of you." Her voice was short, almost brittle. She had deep lines at her mouth and the corners of her eyes.

She wasn't feeling well, Blake thought, and even though Billy had warned her not to discuss her arthritis with her, Blake couldn't help but be concerned. "Are you in pain?" she asked.

Summer slowly sat down at the table. "Nauseous, more than anything."

"Can I make you some tea, or toast? Would crackers help?"

"A different medicine would help." Summer sagged, shoulder slumping. "I can move better, but what's the point when you feel worse?"

"What medicine are you taking?" Blake asked.

Summer gave her the name. Blake knew of it, but wasn't as familiar with it as she would have liked.

"I've been seeing a new doctor," Summer added. "He put me on some new meds, but I think the side effects are worse than the treatment. I'm constantly queasy. I've gained weight on it. Have terrible headaches. It puts me in a poor mood."

"I've been on medicine that made me nauseous, and it's hard to enjoy life when you feel sick all the time." Blake rose and went to the stove, put on the teakettle. Summer hadn't said yes to tea, but she also hadn't said no. Maybe a mint or peppermint tea would help settle her stomach. Once the burner was on, she turned to face Tommy's mother. "There might be something else you can take, something that would have fewer side effects. You should explore that with your doctor."

"I don't find Freckles easy to talk to. He's a little high and mighty. Wants to tell me what I need to take and then he's done, and I'm being hustled out."

"That's probably because medical practices today have a quota of patients doctors must see. Surveys have shown that the average appointment time is between ten minutes and eleven minutes, which really isn't very long to spend with a patient, get information, check in on how they're feeling, and make a diagnosis."

"I used to like our family doctor, Dr. Giddings. He took care of all the boys. He used to take care of me. But then he didn't seem to know the newest treatments for rheumatoid arthritis and Billy and Tommy insisted I see one of the new specialists at the hospital complex. And yes, Freckles knows about new treatments, but I miss the way Dr. Giddings listened. He always made me feel important. I don't feel important anymore. I feel like a foolish old lady with too many problems."

"Well, that's this new doctor's fault, not yours. And you don't have too many problems. People age, that's just part of life, and you are aging, but that's not a bad thing. Aging is natural. It's what we do. You deserve better care than what your new doctor is giving you. And if you're not happy with the doctor you're seeing in Marietta, there have to be other specialists close by. Bozeman isn't that far. I'm sure you'd have a lot more options there."

"I hate to trouble the boys, or Sophie. She's always so good at taking time off of work to drive places Joe or Melvin can't. You know, I don't drive anymore."

Blake suppressed her smile. "Yes, I didn't expect you are still driving. Do you miss it?"

"I do. I really enjoyed the freedom of getting in my car, driving into Marietta, buying groceries at a big grocery store, walking around downtown, doing some window shopping. It was a treat to slip away, while the boys were in school, have a little time to myself. I used to go into town once a month to get my hair done. I really enjoyed that."

The more Blake talked to Tommy's mom, the more she liked her. "I'm sure Sophie doesn't mind taking time off of work to drive you places." The teakettle whistled and Blake turned off the heat and then looked through the cabinet, and yes, there was a box of herbal mint tea. She found a cup, dropped in the tea bag and poured hot water over the tea. "From what Tommy said, Sophie comes from a close-knit family. It probably makes her feel good to take you on errands."

Blake carried the teacup to the table, and set it down in front of Summer. "Do you like honey and lemon? Or…"

"Honey, please. It's in that little bear over there near the coffeepot."

Blake found the plastic bear, located a spoon, and returned to the table, taking her seat and handing both to Summer. "Are you sure you wouldn't like some toast?"

Summer shook her head. "Thank you, this is lovely. Much appreciated." She took her spoon to the tea, pushed it around a bit. "We're all hoping Tommy will settle here. We're hoping once he's off the circuit, he'll return permanently, help Joe. Billy has his own place in Utah. Sam has a ranch with Ivy, twenty minutes from here. Melvin won't be around forever, and this is a big ranch for one person, even with a half dozen hired hands. Besides, my boys grew up doing everything together. Joe can be a bit bossy and impatient with his younger brothers, but he's always gotten along well with Tommy. Maybe that's because Tommy's easygoing, and funny, and Joe takes everything so seriously."

Summer removed the tea bag, added a little bit of honey, and stirred. "But then, Joe was seven when his dad died, and from seven on, he thought he had to be the man of the family. That's a lot of pressure for a little boy, especially one that adored his daddy. Joe was a daddy's boy, through and through."

The idea of four little boys losing their dad put a lump in Blake's throat. "Can't even imagine how awful that must have been."

"Was terrible. The boys actually bounced back better than me. I was broken for a long time. The first year I was here, I could barely get out of bed. Melvin earned his angel wings then, that's for sure. There he'd lost his only sons, and then suddenly he was having to take care of four little boys, and a heartbroken me. That man has broad shoulders, but he shouldn't have had to take on so much."

"Maybe that's what has kept him so young, having all of you here. I get the impression that he enjoys his grandsons… and you." Blake hesitated. "What was his wife like? Has he been a widower long?"

"She died early in their marriage, when the boys were quite young. Leukemia, I believe. He's never talked about it, and JC never talked about his mom very much. I always got the impression that he didn't have a lot of good memories of her. Probably wasn't pretty, seeing her waste away."

Blake suddenly felt as if she'd throw up. Light-headed, she sat back and very still, drawing slow breaths.

And that was why she'd never have children.

That pretty much summed up everything.

She sipped her coffee, discovered it had grown cold. She crossed the kitchen, going to the microwave to reheat her cup. When the thirty seconds were over, she turned to Summer, a smile firmly in place. "Was it hard for you to adjust to Montana? After all, you were a Californian."

"The weather can be harsh. The summers are beautiful, some years we have a nice long summer, and some years it's on the short side, but living in all this beauty makes up for it. Grass Valley was at the base of the Sierra Nevadas, and I like mountains. Here, I'm surrounded by mountains, and every season has its beautiful colors. I didn't come from an affluent family, and never had a lot of emotional support from Mom or Dad, so moving here to be on the Wyatt ranch was the right thing to do. Melvin's a good man, a devoted dad, devoted grandfather. He knew what to do with all of us. I didn't."

Tommy walked through the kitchen door then, followed closely by Melvin. They took off their hats and coats, hanging them on iron hooks by the door.

"Granddad and I are thinking of making some eggs.

We're hungry. Who wants to eat?" Tommy asked.

Blake was still leaning against the counter, in front of the microwave. She flashed back to the night before, and how she'd fallen asleep in his arms, with him just rocking her.

Tommy was like Melvin. Steady, loving, loyal, giving.

What a good man he was.

Her eyes stung, and her throat ached.

He looked at her, smiled. "Hungry?" he asked.

She nodded, unable to look away from him. He was so unbelievably handsome—he was always handsome—but right now, in this moment, she didn't think she'd ever seen anyone more gorgeous, or more alive. The morning chill had made his blue eyes brighter, and his face was ruddy, his straight white teeth flashing in his easy smile.

"Yes," she said, clasping her cup, savoring the warmth.

"Good," he said, turning to Summer. "How about you, Mom? Want some breakfast?"

"I'm fine," Summer said. "Maybe a slice of toast." She nodded at Blake. "It was the doctor's suggestion."

Tommy and Melvin both looked at Blake and she felt the oddest emotion—love, but also grief. It was all bundled up together in this raw knot of hot sensation.

She could be happy here. She could live here and love these people and never want to leave.

To be part of them, to be loved by them.

To love them in return.

Tommy was hopeful and good. Brave and strong.

In Las Vegas, she'd fallen for him that very first night, and she felt the same love now. The love was still huge. Overwhelming.

"I could make the toast," Blake said, aware that the attention was still focused on her. "I'm good at toast, but terrible with eggs. You won't want eggs if I make them."

"You don't know how to make eggs?" Summer asked, astonished.

Blake shook her head. "I'm not much of a cook. My mom always liked to be the one at the stove. But it's time I learned, I know. I don't think you're a grown-up until you know how to make proper scrambled eggs."

Tommy moved to her side, kissed her brow, and went to the sink to wash his hands. "I think graduating med school and finishing your residency proves you're a competent adult," he said, soaping his hands as if a doctor prepping for surgery. "I wouldn't worry about the egg part. Certainly doesn't bother me, since I'm very good at it."

She handed him a towel and smiled. He took it from her but didn't let her hand go. For a moment, he just held her hand in the towel, and his gaze met hers and held. Electric awareness shot through her, making her exquisitely sensitive from head to toe. She'd give anything for just a kiss from him… to be held the way he'd once held her.

She couldn't look away from him. In that moment, no one else was there. It was just them, together.

And right now, like this, everything made sense. Being

with him was heaven. Yes, that's what this was. Heaven.

After breakfast, Tommy and Melvin returned to work, and Blake opened her laptop at the dining room table and studied. She was still studying when Tommy came in and told her that he had plans for them. "It's a beautiful day," he said. "I was thinking we could go for a drive, show you Paradise Valley. Maybe even head into Yellowstone if we're up for it."

"Sounds great." She immediately saved up her work and closed the laptop. "Should I make us a lunch we could take? I'm sure you're going to be hungry soon."

"I thought we'd go to one of my favorite places in Gardiner for lunch, but the picnic is a good idea. It's what my grandparents used to do. I'll tell you more later. I'll be out front waiting. No hurry. I'm not leaving without you."

She was upstairs in her room, changing her shoes and grabbing a sweater when she heard a deep engine and looked out the window with its view of the driveway and there was Tommy pulling up in a pale blue convertible, the blue the color of a robin's egg. The roof was down, the interior was a creamy white. And Tommy had swapped his cowboy hat for a baseball cap and sunglasses and looking down on him, she thought he looked like a movie star.

Blake grabbed her sunglasses, purse, and raced down the stairs. Tommy was talking to his mom and granddad when she stepped through the front door onto the porch. Tommy had prepared her for all seasons, but today was gorgeous and warm. The sky was blue, the sun was shining, and the vintage Cadillac with fins and a bullet grill was in mint condition, the paint glossy and the chrome gleaming.

"Oh, that's beautiful," Blake said, walking to the car. She glanced from convertible to Tommy and then Melvin. "Is this another one of yours, Mr. Wyatt?"

Melvin nodded. He was clearly proud. "You like it?"

"It's amazing."

"I'll have to show you my cars before you leave… but only if you like them. Not everyone appreciates the classics."

"What year is it?" she asked.

"It's a 1960 Cadillac Deville."

"Wow." She looked over at Tommy. "Are we really driving in this? Won't the mountain roads be hard on it?"

"Cars are meant to be driven," Melvin said firmly. "And it's a warm, dry day, perfect to take it out. We should get it out once more before I let it go."

"You're selling it?"

"Can't hang on to all the cars and trucks forever." Melvin ran his hand over the back fin. "Although this one is special."

Tommy looked at her, gave her a nod, making her think he'd tell her more later. "Should we go?"

"Can't wait." She held up her sweater. "Will this be enough?"

"I've given Tom some blankets," Summer said. "I know you're going to lunch, but I'm sending some drinks and snacks. It's all in the trunk."

Summer and Melvin stood on the front steps of the house, waving them off.

Blake leaned on the door and waved back. "I feel like we're pioneers heading across the country instead of going for an afternoon drive."

Tommy shot her an easy smile. "It's an awfully big send-off for an afternoon drive, but they're just happy to see the Cadillac out."

"Or perhaps they're happy to see you happy?" she said, settling back. She was excited to be heading off, just the two of them. She hadn't realized it until now, but she'd been craving time alone with him, craving more closeness and connection.

"Mom has a bit of a soft spot for me," he admitted.

"But not your granddad?" she teased.

"Okay, they both do, but that's maybe because I'm the youngest."

"Or because you're lovable."

"I am, aren't I?" he answered, glancing at her, a wicked gleam in his eye.

She laughed.

He patted the big creamy white bench seat. "There's a middle seat belt," he said. "Slide over. Come sit closer to me."

She did and fastened the middle belt. They now sat hip to hip, thigh to thigh. It was better than nice. She felt giddy. Alive.

"It's such a beautiful day," she said a few minutes later, sighing with pleasure. The air was so fresh, the temperature not hot, but not cold, and the jagged mountains against the very blue sky kind of took her breath away. "I had no idea Montana was so pretty."

"The state is filled with mountains. That's where the name Montana comes from."

"And this weather!"

"It is nice," he agreed, "but I think it's coming to an end."

She scanned the cloudless blue sky. "Really? It's perfect right now."

"Granddad and I were listening to the news this morning. A front is moving in. Wind, rain, colder temperatures."

"Oh, I hope not." She raised her arms over her head, reaching for the sunshine. "This is glorious."

He glanced at her, lips quirked. "Have you been able to get any studying done?"

"Quite a bit actually."

"You're not feeling neglected?"

"Not at all. Your mom kept an eye on me today. She made me tea, with a bit of honey, and even put a lemon cookie on my plate."

"She likes you."

"She likes everyone."

Tommy made a rough sound. "No. No, she most definitely does not. She hasn't been easy on some of the other new wives"—he glanced at her, quickly adding—"obviously not my wives, but when Sophie first arrived here, Mom was pretty tough on her."

"Why?"

"She found out that Joe advertised for a wife and Sophie answered the ad—"

"*What?*"

He navigated a curve in the steep mountain road, driving through a cluster of trees and emerging on the other side into sunshine.

As they left the shade he glanced at her, lips curving. "They're madly in love now, but they didn't start out as a love match. They both wanted family, kids, but they weren't looking for romance, and then they fell for each other, and are pretty perfect together."

"If Joe is anything like you, why advertise for a wife? I'd think women would be into him."

Tommy hesitated. "He had someone he loved very much, and she loved him, but she couldn't face living here instead of in town, and they'd break up, and then they'd get back together again, but then they broke up and she found someone else, and he was devastated when she married. He swore off love."

"Who was this person? Is she still around?"

"Yes. And they're friends now, but that's in part because Sophie smoothed things over. I don't think Joe and Charity will ever be close, but at least they can be comfortable in the same room."

"I want to meet Sophie."

"They should be here in a few days, before you return home."

"Billy said she's from California's Central Valley?"

"From a Portuguese dairy family in Tulare County. She worked in a fruit import/export business after college. She's pretty badass. Joe isn't easy, and Sophie is one of the few people that can handle him."

Blake laughed, amused. "Is there a secret to handling difficult Wyatts?"

"I am not a difficult Wyatt. I am the easiest of them all."

"I'll have to ask your mom about that. I think she'll tell me the truth."

He laughed, and as they descended the mountain and Tommy turned south on Highway 15, Blake closed her eyes for a moment, and just absorbed the sun and the warmth. With the wheels of the Cadillac humming on the road, and the air blowing through the car, she felt as if the sun was kissing her cheeks, soothing her, making her feel good. Free.

It had been so long since she'd felt free.

Her life was filled with work and discipline and, yes, she was a driven person and ambition wasn't bad, but it was hard for her to relax, hard to just let go and be. Maybe she could just be right now. Maybe she could just be mortal and fragile and know how short time was, how fleeting it all was.

Maybe she could hold this moment inside of her, hold the joy and banish the pain.

Maybe God wouldn't mind if she just let go of her control and gave it up to Him. Maybe...

Tommy's hand settled on her leg and she opened her eyes, glanced at him. His attention was on the road, but he seemed relaxed and happy, too.

Blake covered his hand with hers and just left it there. It felt so good to be touching, skin against skin. It was such an innocent touch but she felt the warmth and comfort all the way through her.

Maybe just for today, she could let herself truly love him. Maybe just for today, she didn't have to think about the future and reality and what was to come. Maybe today, they could both just be happy.

What did her mom used to say? *Don't worry about tomorrow, for tomorrow will worry about itself.*

"You okay?" he asked a few minutes later, his voice deep, raspy.

She linked her fingers through his. "Yes. And you? Are you okay?"

"It's a beautiful day, I've got my girl, and we're taking a drive in a very cool car. What more could a guy need?"

She gave his fingers a squeeze and looked past him at the rugged landscape with its backdrop of mountains and the dark blue Yellowstone River rushing on their left.

What more could a girl need?

They drove to Gardiner, and then on to the north entrance of Yellowstone. "Feel like seeing if we can spot any buffalo?" he asked, slowing as they approached the park entrance.

"I'd love to." But then she looked at the car. "They won't... attack, will they? We're in a convertible."

"Just don't stand up and shout and wave your arms," he answered.

She looked at him quickly. "Really?"

"No." He laughed. "We'll be fine. We'll just drive to Lamar Valley and turn around."

They did end up seeing buffalo, hundreds of them actually, big herds grazing in the distance, as well as several smaller herds closer to the road. In one spot, traffic had stopped because a herd decided to cross the road, and everyone was leaning out the window, taking pictures.

"Sit still, and stay calm," Tommy said as the buffalo were moving. "We have one coming up from behind us. It'll be passing on your right very soon."

Blake looked into her rearview mirror, and Tommy hadn't been exaggerating. An enormous buffalo with a huge head and huge horns was slowly walking along the road, passing cars and approaching the Cadillac's bumper.

Her heart raced as she listened to the thudding of footsteps. Dirt rose, clouding the air, and she could hear the buffalo's breathing.

She squeezed as close to Tommy as she could and reached out to take his hand. "What if he puts his head in the car?" she whispered. "What if he—" She broke off as the buffalo drew even with the Cadillac. His ear flicked as he glanced at them, but dismissed them, and he continued on his way, a giant shaggy beast that took her breath away.

Once the bison were done crossing the road, traffic began to move again, too. People were still taking pictures and it was only then that Blake realized she hadn't taken any on the trip so far. But maybe that was good. Maybe just being in the moment was the important thing.

Her heart was still pounding as Tommy shifted into drive. A few miles later he made a U-turn at a turnout for a hiking trail, and they started back for Gardiner. The bison herd that had crossed in front of them was now happily grazing off to the left, moving along the river banks.

"That was one of the most amazing things I've ever seen," she said, before pointing to an enormous male moving slowly at the back of the herd. "Isn't that our buffalo?"

Tommy lifted her hand to his mouth, kissed it. "It is."

"Incredible."

They drove in contented silence until leaving the park where Tommy asked if she wanted to stop and eat. "There's a great place here for buffalo burgers and huckleberry shakes," he said.

"I am hungry," she admitted, "but I can't eat a buffalo burger after our drive."

"We're not eating protected animals. These have been raised on a ranch for consumption—"

"Okay, but we don't have to talk about it, do we?"

She didn't order a buffalo burger, or a hamburger, choosing grilled trout while Tommy had what he wanted. She tried his huckleberry shake and it was good, but she was happy with her water. When she'd finished eating, she was reminded of something she saw him do several days ago. "Tommy, I noticed at the airport you were reading *Travels with Charley* by Steinbeck. Did you know Steinbeck was from Salinas? He graduated from Salinas High School."

He used his paper napkin to wipe his mouth, and then his hands. "I did know. It was why I was reading Steinbeck. I've read most of his other work. *Travels with Charley* has been on my list for a while."

"Do you read a lot?" she asked, surprised.

"I try to. I like to read writers from where I'm competing, and as I've spent the past ten years on the road, it's given me a unique perspective on America."

"When do you read?"

"Usually in the afternoon, during breaks between training and competing, or appearances and events. I don't read fast, usually takes me a week to get through a book—"

"That's pretty fast."

He shifted at the picnic table, stretching his long legs out. "I know I haven't been to college. I'm very aware that I haven't been to college, it's probably one of my biggest regrets, and so I'm always challenging myself to learn things so I can be informed, and I don't mean just with current events, either. I pay attention to the stock market and the US economy. I read the *Wall Street Journal*. I listen to podcasts about economics. There are a number of different sources I go to for information. I think it's important not to listen to just people on one side of the political spectrum, or the other. I think it's important to listen to people. To be an American. To care about everybody. At least that's the way I was raised. Granddad has always said love first, ego last. And so, it's not important if someone is right or wrong. What's important is to act out of love."

*What's important is to act out of love.*

Blake's chest tightened. What a beautiful sentiment, one expressed so clearly not just by Melvin, but by Tommy.

She reached across the picnic table and took his hand, holding it tightly, feeling as if he was holding her heart in his. She still loved him so much. Not just love as in loving him, but as *in* love with him.

"Still my hero," she said huskily. "Still all things good and great."

"Not great," he answered, his thumb stroking the back of her fingers. "Just a guy who is going to seize this week and make the most of it."

Blake's gaze met his and held. "You're making my heart hurt."

"Why?"

"We know how this week ends."

"The week isn't over."

"But when it is, you'll keep your promise to me?"

"I gave you my word, only, it's not the end of the week yet, which means, I'm still playing to win."

"Oh, Tommy."

"Don't feel sorry for me, sweetheart. I'm okay. I know what I'm doing."

She wasn't convinced, and she did worry for him. "When I leave, I don't want you to be sad. When this is over, you have to move on. You have to take care of yourself. You have to find someone who will be a good partner for you. You deserve that, Tom. You deserve the best things, and the best woman, and the best love."

His eyes searched hers. "Why can't that be you?"

Her lips parted, but she couldn't find words.

He stood up and came around to straddle the bench she was sitting on. "Why aren't you those things? I don't think it's because you are a doctor and you work long hours. That's nonsense."

He was so close to her she could see tiny flecks of silver in his blue eyes. "Because I am a doctor. Because I'm not as good as you at juggling responsibilities."

"I don't believe that for a moment."

She didn't know how to do this. She didn't know how to deter him. Short of coming up with huge lies, she didn't know how to make any of this makes sense.

And she didn't want to lie to him. Lies would make it all worse.

She leaned forward, touched his cheek, savoring the texture of his skin and the roughness of his jaw. She leaned even closer, her eyes locked with his, and then ever so slowly she pressed her lips to his. It was supposed to be a brief kiss, but the moment her lips touched his, time slowed and she breathed him in, breathing in his smell and his warmth, and the way sensation streaked through her, pleasure, desire.

Just like the first kiss in Vegas, it was electric. She felt electric, as if she'd been plugged into a socket, white hot energy racing through her, through him, making her tingle, sensitive, so sensitive.

Gently, she raked her nails over his jaw even as he deepened the kiss, his tongue teasing her upper lip. The pleasure was heightened by her emotions. She needed this, wanted him, wanted everything she'd denied herself since leaving Las Vegas three years ago.

But even as her body and heart responded, the laugh of a child punctured her haze of desire, reality returning in a rush. Blake sat up swiftly, cheeks hot, heart pumping. Her nape still prickled, her body felt treacherously warm. Electric desire still pulsed through her as she stared into Tommy's blue eyes.

His eyes glowed, hot, bright. She could feel his hunger. See his love. His need. How hard this must be for him. How hard for him to just wait, to have so little control.

Her eyes burned and stung, tears pricking the back, making her blink. Blink hard. Carefully, she pushed a wave of blond hair back from his brow. "That was good," she said hoarsely.

To be fair, it was better than good. The kiss was perfection. He was still magic, his lips making her feel a thousand different things. She looked up into his eyes, and she was lost. Three years and three months since she'd last kissed anyone.

Three years and three months since she'd been loved.

She hadn't thought she'd missed kissing until now. Blake dropped her hand, stroked a straight eyebrow, and then the bridge of his nose, and finally his mouth. He had this gift for making her feel like a whole, healthy woman.

Warm, sensitive, emotional, hopeful.

Strong.

"Have you been practicing?" she whispered.

He tucked a curl behind her ear. "No. These lips have been saved for yours."

"Me, too."

He arched an eyebrow. "You haven't kissed your Kendrick?"

She lightly punched his arm. "He's not my Kendrick."

"He would be, if you let him."

"Do we have to talk about him?" she asked, growing exasperated.

"I suppose we could kiss some more," he said.

She laughed and glanced around the restaurant's patio, seeing the families and couples enjoying lunch and the sunshine. "Yes, but maybe not here. We have an audience."

He looked around, noted the children. "Okay, it's a little public," he agreed. Tommy stuck some bills beneath his plate and rose, holding a hand out to her. "Let's get out of here."

On the way home, Blake sat as close to Tommy as she could, her hand on his hard thigh, feeling his warmth and strength, trying not to remember how it had felt when they'd made love. Trying not to want that intimacy again. It wouldn't help her leave if she let him get that close. But, oh, she'd missed him. She'd missed him more than anyone would ever know.

# CHAPTER EIGHT

CLOUDS MOVED IN overnight. It wasn't significantly colder the next morning, but the wind was gusting and gray clouds were starting to bank overhead.

Tommy and Melvin were heading out for a ride to check on a windmill that had stopped turning and invited Blake to join them as it was a relatively easy ride. Blake declined, explaining she'd never been on a horse before and didn't want to hold them back. But Melvin said it was a perfect time to try, as Summer's horse was old and gentle, and would be happy to just follow behind one of the lead horses, and that being on horseback gave one a different appreciation of the land. After that, Blake didn't feel as if she could refuse, so she dressed in jeans and her warm hiking boots, T-shirt and sweatshirt.

Summer eyed Blake's attire as she returned to the kitchen. "No cowboy boots?" she asked Blake.

"I have a pair that Tommy bought me in Las Vegas but they're really pretty—they have red and pink roses stitched on them—and I don't want to get them muddy."

"Those don't sound like work boots," Summer agreed,

looking down at Blake's feet. "What size do you wear?"

"Seven."

Summer turned to Tommy. "Go get her a pair of boots from my closet. I'm a seven and a half, but she can put on thick socks. She'll appreciate having boots in the stirrups. Also, make sure she has a heavier jacket, to block out the wind."

Blake wasn't about to argue with Tommy's mom, and when Tommy returned with a pair of worn, but clean cowboy boots, and a heavy canvas jacket, she put both on.

Melvin had already saddled Jenny for her, and gave her a hand, helping to hoist her into the saddle. "The grandkids usually ride Jenny now," he said, adjusting the stirrup on one side, and then the other.

"How many grandkids are there?" she asked.

Tommy answered. "Billy has a toddler, Joe and Sophie have two but I think she's pregnant again, and Ivy and Sam have two-year-old twins, so five grandkids at the moment."

"Christmas around here must be fun."

"Chaotic but wonderful," he agreed.

"And your mom is good with all the little people?"

"She's a softie," Melvin said.

Tommy nodded. "She's waited her whole life for grandkids. I'm sure she's going to make a comment to you about wanting kids from me soon. Don't let it throw you. She's a bit obsessed about me settling down, becoming a dad. But there's time." His gaze met hers, held. "Lots of time. So, no pressure, okay?"

Blake's heart turned over, more troubled than grateful. She couldn't have kids. Nor would she be adopting.

Fortunately, there was no time to dwell on the subject as Melvin gave her a quick riding lesson—teaching her how to hold the reins, guide the horse, sit in the saddle, make Jenny go, slow, and stop. Jenny was so sweet and patient through Blake's training that Blake reached down to pat Jenny's shoulder and tell her what a lovely horse she was. Then they were off, riding down a dirt road, past the barn and paddock, past outbuildings. Melvin pointed out the smaller barn which housed his cars. Another riding ring sat between the big barn and the smaller barn. Melvin said that the boys practiced there in good weather, but in poor conditions they used the ring inside the big barn.

Blake had no idea there was even an arena inside the big barn. She realized she hadn't ventured outside on the ranch much. Perhaps she should have tagged along with Tommy on some of his chores just to see what life here was like. Initially she hadn't wanted to know too much, not wanting to get too involved, or attached, to Tommy's world, but it was too late for that. She rather adored Melvin. He was such a strong patriarch, and so kind to her. Summer was fascinating, and Blake respected her as well. Tommy's family were good people, and he was good people.

During the ride to the windmill, Blake was amazed at different things—the creak of the leather saddle, her lack of core muscles, and how her thighs chafed after just an hour's ride. Even though Jenny was surefooted and calm, when they went to cross a creek, Jenny balked a bit, or maybe Blake balked, or Jenny felt Blake's fear, but Jenny turned sideways and Blake yanked on the reins and then Jenny did another circle, rearing up in confusion, splashing water.

Blake managed to stick—just barely—but she was shaken by the time they crossed the creek. "That was scary," she told Tommy, who'd rode up quickly, caught Jenny's bridle and helped guide Jenny across the creek when she no longer wanted to go.

"You did great," he said, leaning over and kissing her.

She suddenly felt much better about being almost thrown. "What did I do wrong?" she asked.

"You probably needed to be a bit firmer about your intention to cross. You might have pulled back on the reins a bit or given mixed signals. At the same time, Jenny might have just been stubborn. It happens."

Probably not to him, she thought.

They reached their destination, a tall, three-legged metal windmill, which used the wind to create energy, lifting underground water to the surface for crops, as well as water for livestock. Tommy and Melvin dismounted to inspect the windmill rods, and when that didn't seem to be the issue, Tommy climbed the ladder to the top, and checked the gears there.

Blake tried to be nonchalant, but it was hard not to stare.

Tommy was seriously sexy working. He knew what he was doing, and he made it all look easy.

Tommy wasn't a city boy. He was meant for this kind of life. It suited him and brought out the best in him. He'd been raised working with his grandfather, and he'd learned well. He belonged here, a Wyatt carrying on the Wyatt name.

They returned to the house a half hour later. This time Blake made sure Jenny followed close behind Tommy's horse, not giving Jenny too much lead. When they reached the barn, she wanted to stay to help with the horses, and she did her best to groom Jenny the same way Tommy was grooming his. It was actually rather soothing, brushing the horse. Jenny was warm and solid. She also affectionately nuzzled Blake. When Blake went upstairs to shower and change, it crossed her mind that for a girl who'd never left the city before, she was doing okay here on the Wyatt ranch. So far, she was holding her own.

Back at the house, after taking a hot shower to warm up, Blake dressed in jeans, a T-shirt, and one of Tommy's red flannel shirts. Going downstairs, Blake spotted Mrs. Wyatt slowly moving around the kitchen with her walker. The kitchen smelled amazing—something delicious was roasting in the oven.

"Is there anything I can do to help you?" Blake asked Summer. "You shouldn't have to be making dinner for all of us, not on your own."

"It's just an easy roast tonight. Melvin already put it in the oven for me. Tommy just finished peeling the potatoes and carrots. You don't have to worry about a thing."

"I wish you would have told me you needed help. I wouldn't have rushed off to the shower."

"You're our guest."

"But I want to help. It makes me feel good." Blake looked around the kitchen, and then peeked into the dining room. "Can I set the table?"

"That would be nice. I think you know where everything is now. But the good dishes for dinner are in the hutch in the dining room. Silverware is in that drawer there, next to the dishwasher. I already have place mats on the table."

"You don't use the dishwasher though."

"When it's just Dad Wyatt and me, there's no point."

Blake paused. "Was it hard, living up here, the only female in the family for so many years?"

"I had good boys. We took care of each other."

"You raised really good boys. I'm quite fond of one of them."

"You and Tommy know each other long?"

Blake was already in the dining room when Summer asked the question and she focused on putting the plates around the table before answering. As she returned to the kitchen she said, "We met over three years ago, in Las Vegas. During the National Finals Rodeo. I was there for a bachelorette party for one of my college roommates. Tommy and I crossed paths, and here we are today."

Summer used her walker to support her as she eased into a chair at the round table. "Was that the year he took his first national All-Around Cowboy title?"

"Yes."

"Were you there?"

"I was. For the last two nights of it. I met him on Thursday, just after he'd finished competing."

"What was his pickup line?"

Blake laughed. "He didn't really have one."

"No? Surely he said something."

"Well, he did." Blake's cheeks felt hot. "He asked if the four gentlemen following me were bothering me."

Summer looked at her expectantly.

Blake nodded. "They were."

"He scared them off did he?"

"His fists did, yes."

"All four? Or did some run off?"

"No, he fought all four."

"He's always been a good fighter. But then, the boys can hold their own. Their granddad made sure they knew how to protect themselves. Although to be fair, sometimes when they were younger, they brawled just because they enjoyed it." She shook her head, but she didn't seem upset. If anything, Summer struck Blake as proud.

"So, after the fight, what happened?" Summer asked.

"He walked me back to my room and said good night."

"That was it?"

"And then he sent me flowers. I woke up to four dozen red roses being delivered to my room, and an invitation to breakfast."

"That's a lot of flowers."

"I agree, especially as I was only in town for another couple days."

"And then?"

"We had breakfast, and we-we just kept clicking. I was there for a friend, but only wanted to be with Tommy. That night I went to see him compete. It was amazing. Sam and Billy were also there. I loved watching them. To see all three of their names up on the leader board, one right after the other. Tommy Wyatt. Sam Wyatt. Billy Wyatt. People all around me were talking about them. It was my first rodeo ever, too."

"What an introduction."

"It was like meeting the star quarterback the day before the Super Bowl, and not knowing he was the star quarterback."

"I've always wanted to see the boys compete in Las Vegas, but I don't like crowds, and the stadium is big, isn't it? Attending the NFRs at the Thomas Mack arena would mean a lot of walking."

"There would be handicap access… a VIP cart, or something, that could whisk you from the parking lot to your seat."

"Oh, I'd never draw attention to myself like that. I'm not a VIP, and don't like fuss. The boys are there to compete, not me. Let them focus on what they're in Vegas to do."

"When was the last time you saw one of them compete?"

Summer needed a moment to think. "Probably the Livingston rodeo, about two years ago." She frowned, remembering. "With everything going on in the world, it seems like forever, doesn't it?"

"It's been a strange couple of years, that's for sure." And Blake wasn't even talking about politics or economics, she was thinking of her own life and everything that had happened. "The NFR was impressive, but it was wonderful seeing him in Salinas last weekend. As a fan, you're a lot closer to the action." She didn't mention that she was a lot closer to seeing Tommy almost gored as well. That hadn't been fun.

"When the boys were growing up, we'd go to a lot of the local rodeos. Livingston, Gardiner, Wolf Point, and of course Bozeman and Billings. The boys started young, and once Joe and Sam were riding, Billy and Tommy had to ride, too. After a year or two, they were all competing every weekend. Dad Wyatt took them. He did the training, just as he'd trained my husband, too."

"Tommy said his dad died in a car accident on the way to a rodeo."

"Died with his brother. I suppose the only good part about it, was that they were with each other, until the end.

They were best friends. Sometimes it felt like it was JC and Samuel, and me. The third wheel."

"I've felt that a little bit, when Tommy and Billy are together."

"The Wyatt men can be tough and stubborn, but they know how to love." Summer said nothing for a moment. "I've never shared this with the boys, didn't seem right, but JC and I didn't get to say goodbye, not properly. He'd been on the road for weeks, and I had four little boys, and I was frustrated. I didn't want to be left alone with them for another week, another weekend." Summer looked off, lightly tapping the table with a finger. "We had an argument, and I hung up the phone, angry. He tried to call back, but I didn't take the call." Her fine features tightened, her mouth compressing. "We never talked again."

Blake sagged and leaned against the refrigerator. What a terrible story. Blake could feel the pain in Summer's voice all these years later. "You didn't cause the accident."

"I should have taken the call. I shouldn't have been petty—"

"It wasn't your fault."

Summer looked at her. Her eyes were filmy with tears. "I let my ego get in the way. Such a terrible mistake. I regret it with all my heart."

Blake crossed the kitchen, pulled out a chair at the table and sat down next to Tommy's mother. "You being angry didn't make that accident happen. You were just frustrated that you couldn't be with him."

"I did just want to be with him." Her voice quavered. "I loved him. He was my sun, my moon, my everything." She took a delicate handkerchief from her sweater sleeve and reached up to dab one eye, and then the other. "Joe looked the most like my JC, but Tommy acts the most like him. JC was fun. He made me laugh. He made me believe that no matter what happens, everything was going to be all right."

Blake's chest ached with bottled emotion. Those were words that she might have said about Tommy. "At least you had all those years with him." A tear fell, before she could stop it. "You gave him his boys. How lucky you were, to have his amazing children."

"They've been everything to me. And I do see my husband in them. I see their uncle in them. But at the same time, they are themselves. They're not to live for me. They're to follow their hearts, to chase their own star."

"And have they?"

Summer nodded. "They're all settled, and happy. All but Tommy." She lifted her head, looked at Blake, holding her gaze. "How serious are you and Tommy?"

Blake was caught off guard by the abrupt change of conversation. "Not sure how to answer that one," she said after a long uncomfortable silence. "We've had some ups and downs. But I admire Tommy immensely. I think he's wonderful."

"But you're not sure about him." Summer gave her a

long searching look. "You haven't decided he's the one for you."

"We just have really different lives. I'm in San Francisco, my family's in San Francisco, my parents are getting older. I could never ask Tommy to go there, what would he do in the city? He wouldn't be happy."

"That's true. He's not cut out for city living. What would he do with his horses? Put them on the cable car?"

Blake knew it was a joke. Summer was trying to lighten the mood. Blake smiled weakly. "They'd look awfully silly, wouldn't they?"

"The tourists would go crazy. Imagine all the pictures they'd take for that instant-thing."

"Instagram?"

She nodded. "Do you do that? Have one of those channels?"

Blake checked her smile. "I don't. Don't have time, or interest."

"Hmph." Summer continued to study Blake. "Have you told him how you feel? Does he know he's more committed than you?"

Wow, Summer didn't pull her punches. Blake left the table, opened the silverware drawer, counted out the knives, the forks, the spoons. "We need to have another conversation," she said carefully. "It's just hard to disappoint him."

"Is there someone else?"

Blake looked at Summer from over her shoulder. "If I

didn't love medicine as much as I do, or if Tommy had property in Sonoma, or the Central Valley, it would be different. But the Wyatt ranch is here. The Wyatts are here. And you've been here for generations. I can't take him from that."

"You can't leave your world?"

Blake held the silverware to her chest. Her heart was racing. Her anxiety was rising. She didn't know if Summer would rush to Tommy and tell him all of this, or if this was a confidential conversation between the two of them. "It's not a matter of cutting the cord. I'm not tied to my parents because I'm spoiled. It's rather that I'm grateful. They have sacrificed everything for me. They have made me the focus of their lives, taking care of me when things were hard. You don't just walk away from the people who have loved you your entire life. You don't."

"How were things hard? If you don't mind me asking?"

Blake's eyes burned. She swallowed, gathered her courage. "I had some health stuff, some scares, and no, Tommy doesn't know. But it was serious. And it's not conducive to family life. I never imagined getting married or having kids. For me, my future has always been medicine. Taking care of others, giving back, making sure my life meant something."

Summer looked at her for a long moment. "You're still not telling me everything. But I respect that. In case you're wondering, I won't say anything to Tom. He and I are close, but you have the right to your privacy. I just ask that you don't lead him on. If it's not going to work out between you, better to let him know sooner than later."

Blake nodded. "I agree." She went into the dining room and laid the silverware on the place mats. She came back for the dinner plates, and placed those around the table, too. When she returned to the kitchen for glasses, she saw that Summer had her head down, and was crying.

Blake froze, her chest tightening, the lump in her throat making it hard to breathe. If she didn't know better, she'd think Summer was crying for her, for Tommy, for them.

Blake turned around and walked out and headed up the stairs to her bedroom. Quietly, she closed the door, and sank onto the bed, turning over to bury her face in a pillow.

For the first time in forever, Blake gave in to tears, crying for the future she wouldn't have. She'd only been fifteen when diagnosed with ovarian cancer. Fifteen and she wasn't supposed to make it to eighteen, but she had, and for five years she lived life, seizing every opportunity—college, med school, the impulsive wedding with Tommy—and then in January, just weeks after marrying him, the cancer was back and it had metastasized. It wasn't ever going to go away.

She didn't want anyone but her family to know. It was her battle, and she'd fight until she couldn't, but Tommy couldn't know. If he did, he'd drop everything to be with her and that wasn't fair, not to him. He had a future. He needed to live his future, not watch her die in front of him.

Kendrick knew because he was a fellow student, and

when she couldn't make classes, he'd come to her at the hospital, and then later at home, and study with her. He'd review with her, or sometimes flat out teach her. He was such a good friend. But it was purely platonic. She had no romantic feelings for him. She loved Tommy too much.

She still loved Tommy too much.

This was a mistake, being here. Love meant doing what was best for the other person.

If Blake had learned anything in her life, if she learned anything from her parents' marriage, if she'd learned anything from the sacrifices they had made for her, it was that love wasn't selfish. Love didn't keep track of rights and wrongs, love was the most important thing in the world, but it was also the most consuming.

She couldn't ask Tommy to be in her life. He wouldn't be able to travel; he wouldn't be able to focus on his career. Her needs would eventually supersede his own. And he was too young, too talented to become tied to her. He would resent it, too. Maybe not right away, but eventually.

Even though her parents were her parents, she knew her health and issues had worn them down. She'd heard them having intense discussions when they thought she couldn't hear them. Neither of them blamed her, but fear and worry wore them down, and the financial burden was enormous. They worried about the future. They worried about her. They worried about how they'd manage financially. And so, exhausted, they turned on each other.

A knock sounded on the bedroom door and she sat up and used her sleeve to scrub her face dry. It was Tommy at the door.

"Hey," he said, gaze narrowed, sweeping over her face. "Everything okay?"

She nodded.

"Mom said she might have upset you." Tommy entered the room, closed the door, and wrapped his arms around her, bringing her close. Thigh to thigh, hip to hip, chest to chest. "She is sorry—"

"Nothing to be sorry for," Blake said, huskily, emotions so close to the surface because she was only now realizing she'd never really dealt with her future, or lack of. She'd just closed the door on it, and not let herself think about it, but being here with Tommy, being with his family, made her realize what she'd never have.

Family.

Children.

This closeness, this happiness, this security and safety.

Her eyes filled with tears. "She's a really good person. I like her a lot."

"Why so sad then?" He gently wiped away one of her tears before it fell.

How to tell him she couldn't have babies because she had no ovaries? How to tell him she couldn't adopt because she wouldn't be here to see her children grow up? How to tell him that the only time she wasn't afraid was when she was with him, but because of that, she couldn't confide in him?

"The time is passing quickly, isn't it?" She took her sleeve to blot tears. "It's going to be the weekend soon."

"We don't have to sign the papers," he said. "We don't have to make a decision this week. We can let it ride, circle back around to this later. After three years, why make the final decision now?"

If she told him the truth, he'd never leave her.

If she told him the truth, he'd walk away from every-thing now and spend whatever time was left with her.

But Tommy needed more. He needed a wife who would take care of him. He needed children. He needed a home that was filled with love and laughter, family and traditions. Not grieving.

She wrapped her arms around him and held tight. For just this one moment, she'd love him. She'd pretend she was healthy, she'd pretend the future hadn't yet been written, and they could create the story together. She'd pretend she'd fall asleep with him every night, and wake with him every morning, and they had babies who'd know their great-grandfather Melvin Wyatt, and he'd put their babies on the old mare, Jenny, and walk them around the yard, a hand on their little backs, the sun shining down on their heads, and there would be another generation of Wyatts growing up here on the Wyatt ranch.

That was what she'd have, if she could have any future.

She'd practice medicine somewhere nearby.

She'd come home at night to dinner here, and smile at Tommy from across the dinner table, or better yet, sit next to him so they could hold hands under the table.

They'd sleep close, his arms around her, her leg between his. She'd wake up with him kissing her, and she'd check on their babies and then go downstairs and have coffee with Summer and Melvin—

Blake stopped there.

What about her parents?

Did she just leave them behind?

"I can feel your thoughts race," Tommy murmured, his hand slipping up her back, his palm so warm, so firm against her spine.

"I wish California was closer to Montana."

"It's not that far," he answered. "Just a couple-hour flight."

She pressed her cheek to his chest, breathing in his scent, listening to his heart. "I love you," she said.

His arms held her more tightly. "Still?"

"Always."

"Then why…"

Funny, how in his arms she was always safe. In his arms, she was always home. "Neither of us should have to give up what we love to make our marriage work."

"Not even if one of us wanted to?"

She pushed back a little to look up into his face. "You would hate living in the city. It's crowded and noisy. There's

162

no space. It's not for you."

"And you're certain your parents wouldn't be open to moving?"

"I can't imagine them living anywhere else." She hesitated, her eyes searching his, before reaching up to touch his cheekbone and the angle of his jaw. She'd adored him from the very first conversation when nothing seemed to faze him, when he'd put himself out there, unconcerned about what might happen to him, focused instead on protecting her. He was heroic. Her very own hero. "But maybe… maybe. Who knows? Maybe if they met you. Knew about us. Maybe."

"That's a lot of maybes."

"I know."

"What would they think of me?"

"They'd be surprised."

His gaze darkened, a shadow passing over his features. "Because I'm a cowboy? Uneducated?"

"You haven't been to college, but you're not uneducated."

A light rap sounded on the door. "Dinner," Melvin said, from the other side of the door.

"Coming," Tommy called. His hands moved down Blake's arms, and he gave her hands a squeeze before letting her go. "Let's not keep Mom waiting."

SUMMER APPEARED IN the dining room as Blake cleared the

table. Tommy was already at the sink washing dishes.

She stopped Blake with a light hand on her forearm. "Do I owe you an apology?" she asked Blake. "I think I upset you earlier."

Blake's heart ached and she set the glasses down and gave Summer a hug. "No. Not at all." She straightened, stepped back. "I respect you very much. I think you're a wonderful mom, a wonderful woman."

"Tommy isn't perfect."

Blake smiled. "He's pretty perfect."

"No. He can be stubborn. Very stubborn. He's also very independent, and very competitive."

Blake had seen the stubborn side—him refusing to give up on their marriage—but for the rest? Tommy had been nothing but kind and loving. "He treats me very well. Almost too well."

"He has high standards. He doesn't fall in love easily. But when he loves, he loves forever."

Blake forced a smile, trying not to feel like a traitor. "He's definitely special. You did a good job with that one."

WEDNESDAY MORNING THEY woke to snow. It was just a dusting, and was still falling, but Tommy knew it wasn't going to stick. Temperatures would warm later in the morning and the white stuff would melt, but he suspected Blake would be excited to see it before it was gone and he knocked on her door, waking her up.

"Bundle up," he said. "It's snowing right now. Let's go out for a walk."

"Seriously?" she cried, scrambling up in bed, her apricot pajamas adorable on her.

"Yes, seriously."

She was downstairs in less than five minutes in her jeans and her hiking boots, along with a sweater and a scarf. Tommy had her put an oversized parka over her sweater and zipped it closed for her, and then handed her a coffee, fixed just the way she liked it. He leaned against the stove as she sipped it. She still had a crease from her pillowcase on her cheek. Her curls were wild. Her eyes reminded him of the riverbeds, all gold and green.

She looked more gorgeous than he'd ever seen her, and she didn't have a bit of makeup on, no artifice of any kind.

After another big gulp, Blake set her mug down with a *thunk* and smiled at him, teeth so white, happiness contagious. This morning she was like the sun. Bright. Glorious. "Let's go, cowboy."

He laughed, headed for the door, put on his own coat and grabbed his hat. When he opened the door for her, she stepped out and walked to the edge of the covered porch, watching the snow fall.

"Well?" he asked. "What do you think?"

She stuck a hand out, as if to catch a flake, but couldn't quite reach them. He walked down the steps, out into the yard, letting the snow fall around him.

She looked at him for a moment, half smiling. "You look like a prince in a fairy tale," she said.

"Did princes wear Stetsons?"

Her shoulder lifted and fell as she walked down the steps to join him. "I guess in mine they did."

He picked her up off her feet and gave her a spin beneath the soft flurry of white flakes. Snow dusted her curls and when he put her down, he gently wiped a wet snowflake from her cheek. She smiled up at him, her eyes locking with his, and the warmth and desire in his eyes made him ache. He hadn't been planning on kissing her, not now, not here, where his mom and grandfather could see, but once he started kissing her, he couldn't stop, nor did she want him to stop, her arms around his neck, as she kissed him back.

The kiss was hot and fierce even as the snow tumbled past them, tiny icy flakes sticking to their backs and shoulders. They were interrupted by the sound of barking dogs. The dogs meant Granddad would be close behind.

He reluctantly ended the kiss, but didn't let her go. "I've got to help here for a little bit, but then I'm planning on taking you into Marietta for lunch, shopping, maybe a movie. What do you think?"

"Yes. Sounds fun."

He kissed the tip of her nose. "Give me a couple hours and we'll head off." And then, unable to help himself, he kissed her lips again, a slow, lingering kiss, taking advantage of her soft warm mouth and the fire still simmering between them.

Maybe a hotel room would be better than a movie.

But no, he wasn't going to use sex to tie her to him. When they made love, it had been wonderful, intense, explosive, but he wanted her heart this time, not just her body.

THE RANCH WAS still blanketed in a thin layer of white when Tommy and Blake set off for Marietta. Tommy had told her the snow would linger on the ranch as it sat up at a high elevation, but the snow quickly disappeared once they descended into the valley, the fields green, a few daffodils appearing here and there. "It's sunny," she said, turning to Tommy. "I can't believe it was just snowing a couple hours ago."

"Montana weather is a whole thing," he agreed.

They were on the outskirts of Marietta now and he was pointing out landmarks, showing her the turnoff to Miracle Lake, where a miracle reportedly happened one hundred years ago, and one of the big Christmas tree farms, and then the remains of one of the early homesteader cabins.

He'd told her some of the history of the area, and she was excited to see the town itself, especially Bramble House, which had a fabled past, and the courthouse, Grey's Saloon, the historic library, Graff Hotel. Blake wanted to see it all, and after a drive around the town, Tommy parked and they walked Main Street, stopping for a hot chocolate at Copper Mountain Chocolates, where she also picked up a box of chocolates for her mom, and some salted caramels for her dad.

They continued down the street, stopping to admire the window displays of the florist, and an antique shop. Together, they went into the bookstore and browsed. Paradise Books had a huge section on Montana, from travel books to Montana writers. Tommy thumbed through the books until he found what he'd been looking for.

"One of my favorites by Ivan Doig, a Montana novelist. I'm getting this one for you. I know you don't have a lot of time for pleasure reading, but it's a good souvenir."

She stepped close, stood up on tiptoe and kissed him. "Now I can be like you and read about all the places I go."

He tipped her chin up, smiled into her eyes. "We could go to a lot of great places together."

"No doubt."

They had lunch at Grey's Saloon, eating at the bar, with Tommy talking with the bartender, catching up on local happenings. Tommy had introduced her to the bartender as his girlfriend, and the bartender winked at her. "He doesn't date so you must be one amazing girl."

Blake put her hand on Tommy's knee. "This is Tommy Wyatt," she answered. "Champion."

The bartender laughed. "I grew up with that champion.

He's one of the good ones."

"One of the great ones," she corrected.

After lunch, they walked some more, going down Church Street, past the pink hair salon which Sophie helped manage, the dance studio, and the Boys and Girls Club.

"There, on the other side of the street is Dr. Giddings's office," Tommy said.

"Your mom certainly misses him," she answered.

"Or she just detests Dr. Freckles that much more."

Blake laughed and slipped her hand into his as they continued down Second toward Bramble. Once they reached Bramble, Tommy pointed out more houses owned by friends, from the Christmas House to a tall green Queen Anne, and then to Bramble House itself, which had been for sale for six months without a buyer. Someone had made an offer, but just before it closed, the sale fell through.

"It's a gorgeous house," Blake said.

Tommy nodded. "I'd love a house like that."

"It's so big!"

He shot her a teasing smile. "Not if we filled it up with kids."

She kept hold of his hand but her heart fell. This wasn't the first time he mentioned children, and how important they were to him.

Fortunately, they started walking again, continuing their tour past the one hundred-and-twenty-year-old library anchoring the courthouse plaza, and then past the domed courthouse itself.

Behind the courthouse ran a river with a groomed path. Crocuses and daffodils lined the curving path. The path led across a bridge to a large fairground with a new arena. "That's where we used to hold the Copper Mountain rodeo. It hasn't been held in a couple of years but the town is trying to get it going again."

"I imagine you competed here quite a bit growing up," she said.

"I did, along with some fairly big names in the PRCA. I had a lot of heroes compete here."

"And now you're hero to many." She squeezed Tommy's hand, impossibly proud of him. When with him, it was almost as if they'd never been apart. She was so comfortable, so relaxed. She felt like herself—but better. He just made everything better. She pointed to the big building in the distance. "What is that complex?"

His gaze narrowed as he followed her finger. "That's Marietta Medical, our hospital. Recently they've built some additional facilities to accommodate physical therapy and rehab. A number of doctors are moving their practices to the complex, making it easy for patients to be seen all in one place."

"Is that where Dr. Freckles is?" she asked.

Tommy grinned. "Yes. And despite what Mom says, he's a very good doctor. He's just... a little stiff. Takes himself seriously, but that's okay. I'd rather her be seen by someone really good, than a comedian."

"Too bad a doctor can't be both—good at medicine and great with people. Because a compassionate doctor, or a warm doctor, makes a difference. I know."

"We could walk over to the hospital, check it out if you'd like," he said.

She shook her head. "I'd rather visit one of those bakeries on Main Street. Maybe pick up dessert to take home with us?"

"That's a great idea. Let's pick up a cake. Mom and Granddad both love a great chocolate cake."

# CHAPTER NINE

TOMMY WAS WOKEN up by an early morning call from Billy, who was checking in, wanting to know when Tommy would be competing again, and if they were going to be meeting up soon. "Planning on it," Tommy answered. "Joe should be here soon, and once I have my rig, I'll be ready to go."

Billy hesitated. "How is it going there?"

"Good. Mom and Granddad seem to like Blake a lot."

"I meant, how is it going between you and Blake? Will there be wedding bells soon?"

Tommy laughed, but he wasn't feeling as hopeful as he would have liked. He and Blake got along well, very well, but she still wasn't talking about a future, and he didn't know how much harder he could try.

After hanging up, he dressed and headed out of his room. It was still dark out but the hall light was on and his mom was slowly making her way down the stairs. She kept a walker upstairs, and a walker downstairs, and he descended the stairs next to her, just in case she needed him.

"You're up early," he said to her, once she had her walker

and was making her way into the kitchen.

"It was one of those nights," she said.

"Lots of pain?"

"Lots of worries."

He glanced at her as he made coffee. "What are your worries?"

"I thought you were going to take Blake out yesterday. Have a nice dinner."

He paused, gave her a hard look. "That's your worry?"

"You weren't gone very long. Just a few hours."

"We had a nice lunch, explored Marietta, and then we were ready to come home for dinner. Why is that a problem?"

"I just thought you'd want to spend a little more time alone with her. I can't imagine she enjoys being with us old folks all the time."

"You're not old, and Granddad might be old, but he acts younger than Joe."

"The point is, you want to woo your girlfriend. Spoil her. Make her feel special."

He finished making the coffee and pushed brew. "Have a suggestion, Mom?" Tommy asked mildly, amused by his mom's interference. She'd never struck him as a romance expert before.

"Sophie said she and Joe had a nice fondue dinner at the Graff's pub for Valentine's Day. Maybe the Graff is still doing fondue?"

Tommy choked back a laugh. "Fondue, Mom?"

"Women like it," she said, lifting her chin.

"Who knew you were such a romantic?"

"I just think it's important you show her that life could be wonderful when you're not competing. Because you won't always be on the circuit."

"Sam still competes."

"But far less. Now that they have the twins, he's home more and more." She cocked her head, looked at him. "And we both know how much you want a family of your own."

He shifted uneasily. This wasn't something he wanted to discuss with her. There would be a time for children, but he didn't want to try to be a dad when he was always traveling. Billy had to deal with that, and it wasn't a life for him. "Yes, but not yet. Not ready to walk away from the circuit, the money's good. I'm investing everything I can."

"I was surprised you're missing this weekend in Houston."

"Blake was concerned about my concussion. She was adamant I not ride."

"You never listened to me when I said you can't compete."

"She's a doctor."

"And you love her."

He nodded. "I do."

"But it's not just because she's a doctor, is it?"

"I like that she's smart. I respect her ambition. It's important to me that she succeeds."

"You've always been attracted to smart girls."

He didn't reply. There was no need to.

"I'm still hoping you'll go to college," she added. "Who knows? Maybe even earn your master's degree. You always did so well in school. You should have gone to college. The rodeo would have waited."

Tommy honestly wasn't ready for this. He hadn't slept that well himself, and his mom was coming at him fast and hard. "Billy needed a roping partner."

"He and Sam could have been a team, after Joe returned to the ranch. You didn't have to sacrifice your future for his."

He poured himself a cup of coffee even though it hadn't finished brewing, and took a sip. It was hot. It was good. After a moment, he faced his mom. "I haven't sacrificed anything. I've made a lot of money. I'm financially secure. I have formed relationships with all of my sponsors, people willing to continue to invest in me, or any of my future business opportunities."

"You could have been a doctor."

Tommy shuddered. "Would not have enjoyed that, at all. Medicine isn't for me."

"A lawyer then."

"No interest in that, either."

"Then what? Because you're smart, Tommy. You have that amazing head for numbers—"

"Finance. Stock broker—"

"Oh no. They're just salesmen."

"Not all, Mom. Some brokers sell what they're told to sell. Others understand the market." He took a bigger sip of coffee. "I understand the market. I find it fascinating. But I'd also find it interesting working for a company, or with a company, or starting my own. I'm not without ideas." He smiled at her, trying to reassure her. "Don't worry about me. I might be on the circuit now, but I won't be forever."

"Does Blake know that?"

He hesitated. "Why?"

"I'm worried."

"Don't be worried."

"But I am. I just have this feeling that something's… off… between you two. I can't put my finger on it. You clearly care about other, and I've seen you affectionate, but…" Her voice trailed off, and she looked up at him, her brow deeply creased. "There's this worry, and maybe you know something—"

"Is this why you couldn't sleep last night?" he interrupted, reaching for another cup to pour her coffee. "If so, please don't torture yourself. Everything's good. Don't look for trouble where there is none." The last thing he wanted was his mom to worry about him, or for him, especially when there was nothing she could do about their situation.

He carried her the coffee, set it down, and leaned over to kiss her cheek. "But I do think maybe a proper date night might be in order when I'm done working with Granddad.

I'll make a reservation, have a nice, long dinner, and then come home."

Tommy and Melvin spent more time on the property that day than Tommy had expected. The wind had let up, but earlier the gusts had broken limbs on a big tree, and the falling limbs took out part of a fence. Several cattle escaped and so while Melvin fixed the barb wire, Tommy went in search of the missing cows.

It had taken a couple hours to locate the missing three and get them back in the pasture, but all were safe and now he was going to shower and change so he and Blake could leave in time to make their six p.m. dinner reservations.

His mom stopped him on the way up the stairs. "Have you seen Blake?" she asked.

"No. Why?"

"She's in the family room watching the news waiting for you, but she can't go out like that. That poor girl doesn't know how to dress for a date in Montana. She's going to freeze. Ask her if she has anything warmer."

"How is she dressed?"

"A skirt. Blouse. High heels. No stockings, no socks." Summer shook her head. "She's dressed for a date in California. This *isn't* California."

"You don't wear socks with high heels, Mom. I'm sure you remember that rule."

"It's not a matter if I remember fashion rules. It's more of an issue whether you want your girlfriend to get frostbite.

I don't think you do. You're hoping to impress her with a visit to Montana, she won't be happy here if she loses toes while here."

"She's a doctor. She'll put on heavier socks before the toes actually fall off."

"Tom, you're missing the point."

He'd headed up a couple stairs, but came back down to be level with her. "I'm teasing you, Mom. I know the point. But what do you suggest? We borrow some clothes from Sophie? I raid her closet when she isn't looking?"

"No. Just let her know a date night in Marietta is casual. Wear fleece, jeans, thick socks, boots. Tell her she looks beautiful, but she'd be even more beautiful in warm clothes."

"Anything else I should tell my girlfriend?"

Summer cleared her throat. "That you love her."

"She knows."

"Does she?"

"What does that mean?" he asked.

"She doesn't seem happy." Summer hesitated. "She's looked… sad… today. Are you sure everything is okay?"

"She was great when I came in at lunch. She didn't seem unhappy. Maybe something is wrong at home. Please, don't read into it."

"And nothing has happened between you? No fight? No argument?"

"No. But it's also not easy. We're trying to figure out the future. She's interviewing for jobs. My world is here. Her world is there. We're pulled in different directions."

"It's complicated," his mother said.

"Yes," he agreed. "It is."

"And she doesn't want to be a stay-at-home mom while you chase buckles and saddles."

"You didn't like it."

"I'm not criticizing her. It was hard being left behind with babies while your dad competed. I know it was how he made money and paid the bills, but she has different options. She has a career. I didn't."

Tommy had always been close with his mother. His brothers might be able to hide things from her, but he'd never been very good at that. Maybe it was because he was the youngest, and she'd spoiled him a bit more, or maybe it was because he was home with her after the others were gone. He realized she needed support.

"I'm hoping we can work it out," he said carefully. "But if we can't, it's not because I didn't care enough. I honestly couldn't care more."

"In that case, don't think about the end, or the future. Concentrate on today. When you're competing, you don't think about Sunday's events. You think about today's events. This is a Friday at one of your rodeos. You won't even make it to Sunday if you don't do well today."

He leaned over the bannister, kissed her on her forehead. Her skin was delicate, cool. She'd become so fragile over the past few years. "You're a very wise woman, Summer Wyatt."

She reached up, patted his hand where it rested lightly on her shoulder. "You're one of the good ones, Tom. Remember that."

SUMMER HAD TOLD Blake to order the fondue if the Graff still had it on the menu, but the hotel restaurant didn't. Instead, she and Tommy went with the chef's tasting menu, which featured special wine pairings. It was a lovely, leisurely dinner and Blake enjoyed the hotel's old-world elegance.

After dessert had been cleared, Tommy asked for the bill, and then smiled when she yawned a second time. "Not bored," she said quickly, "just full, and very relaxed. We ate a *lot*."

"It was good, though," he said.

She nodded, and reached across the table to take his hand. "Thank you for a lovely night out. This was wonderful. I love your family, but it's nice to just be with you."

"I'm not going to be ready for you to leave," he said, after a moment. "Being with you these past few days reminds me why you're the one for me. I have never loved anyone else, not like this. I will never love anyone else like this either. There is you, and only you."

His words took her breath away. She felt lost in his blue gaze. "I feel the same way."

"Let's not file the paperwork. There's no reason we have to. I don't want anyone else. And you don't want anyone else, do you?"

She shook her head. "No." She swallowed hard. "Not right now, I don't."

He gave her a look that made her insides ache. She'd hurt him. She squeezed his hand. "You made it three years without me. You'll be fine, Tommy. And you'll be free, and you never felt free before, so you never dated, but you should. I can't keep you tied to me. I can't do this to you. Tommy, I love you, but I don't want to be married."

"To anyone or just to me?"

She didn't answer, not right away. She'd never planned on getting married. She never planned on any of this. "To anyone."

"Tell me this," he said, "and I need you to be honest with me. If we never met, and Kendrick had been there, as he is there now, and if he told you how he felt about you, what would happen? Would you be interested in him? Could you see yourself possibly falling in love with him?"

"It's not that simple—"

"He's a good person, isn't he?"

She nodded. "He's very kind. He's compassionate. He's hardworking. He's an excellent doctor. He's someone I admire."

"And so, if you had been free, again, and you had no history with me, and Kendrick asked you out, what would you do? Would you go out with him? Would you want to date him?"

She didn't want to answer this, because it wasn't a real situation. Hypothetical questions didn't hold up to reality. Not her reality. "This is silly. You're stirring the pot, Tommy. Why go there?"

"So your answer would be yes."

"*No.*" She glared at him. "It wouldn't be a definitive yes." She felt breathless, angry, and she released his hand. Her heart was beating so fast. She felt trapped. "It'd be a maybe. And that's the truth. A maybe. Marriage and family was never on the table for me. You were a fluke, Tommy. You weren't supposed to happen, but you did."

He regarded her steadily. "Has your family met him?"

He really wanted to do this? Blake was holding onto her temper by a thread. "Yes."

"They like him."

He said it as a statement, not a question. She gritted her teeth. "They know we go back to med school. They know he's been good for me."

"Are you good for him?"

"*No.* That's just it, Tommy. I'm not good for anyone. I'm not wife material."

"How can you be a good doctor, but not a good wife?"

"As a doctor, I'm married to my work. There is no family life to be sacrificed. There's no one at home waiting for me. There's no one at home worrying about me or are missing me."

"Just your parents."

She said nothing.

"And someday they won't be here anymore. You'd be alone. I don't understand that future. I don't understand how someone like you would *want* a future like that."

"Things have happened in my life, circumstances have shaped me, and if I only have so many years here on earth, I want to do something good with them. I want to give back, instead of just take. I've been so dependent on others these last thirteen years. I don't want to be dependent anymore. I don't want to keep taking."

They left the restaurant quiet. He didn't take her hand, and she didn't reach for his. But once they were in the truck, she slid across the seat, and sat close.

She hated upsetting him, hated disappointing him. Everything had been so good all night, and now this.

Tommy put on some music as he drove back to the ranch. She wished he'd put his arm around her, but he didn't. He was far away, preoccupied. She had a feeling they weren't good thoughts, either.

The drive home hadn't seemed long yesterday, but tonight it went on and on. Her insides churned. She battled her guilt. Battled herself.

As he turned up the long private road leading to the Wyatt ranch, she leaned over and kissed Tommy's cheek, close to his mouth. He smelled of cedar and spice. Just the brush of her lips against his skin filled her with pleasure. Desire.

She loved his skin, his mouth, *him*.

If only the world would freeze, and time would stop, and they could always be here, like this. "Thank you," she said huskily. "Dinner was lovely."

He glanced at her, the light of the dash reflecting his blue gaze. "It was, wasn't it?"

"I have so much fun with you," she said, putting her hand on his leg. "It's like a dream, and I never want to wake up."

"But it's not a dream. It could be like this every day. We just have to choose each other."

A lump filled her throat, making it hard to think, to breathe. Emotions were hot, wild. Tommy made it sound so easy.

But maybe it was that easy.

Maybe she stopped trying to protect him. Maybe she just threw caution to the wind. Why not? He did that every time he got on the back of a bull. He lived in the moment, playing the odds, believing he'd win.

But in her case, she wouldn't win. In her case, she was already living on borrowed time. She pressed her hand against his denim covered thigh. "Just know," she said, voice pitched low, "that no matter what happens, I choose you. And I've always chosen you."

IN HIS ROOM that night, Tommy replayed her words over

and over in his head. *No matter what happens, I choose you. No matter what happens...*

What did they mean, and why? He was beyond frustrated. It felt like they were playing a game now, or at least, she was. And he could do many difficult things, but game playing wasn't one of them.

It was time for honesty. Transparency. But if he wasn't going to get that, he wasn't sure how to make this work. For the first time, he began to think maybe this wasn't going to work out the way he'd hoped.

Maybe this wasn't the future he'd wanted.

Maybe it was time to begin letting go.

Tommy wasn't a quitter. He couldn't remember the last time he gave up on anyone or anything, but he didn't know what was true anymore. Didn't even know who he was anymore. Blake was gorgeous and brilliant and clearly passionate about medicine, but he needed something for him. He needed...

He swallowed hard, hating that he felt these feelings in the first place, but he needed more.

There. He'd said it, put it out there into the universe. But it was true. His truth. It had taken him a long time to get to this point—three years, three months—but he needed more.

Admitting he needed more wasn't easy. It made him feel weak. He spent so much of his life being strong and strong for others, and he could be strong for others, when they were loyal.

He doubted Blake's loyalty.

That was hard to say, but he doubted her loyalty to him. To them. He was a family man, first. Last. In his world, love wasn't a word, it was an action. Love was faith in action. Love was doing what was best for others.

Blake said she loved him, but there was always a dozen reasons why they couldn't be together, why they didn't work, why, why, why she needed to be in San Francisco.

Her work. Her parents. Her guilt.

Kendrick.

Tommy's jaw hardened, his gut knotting as if he'd swallowed rocks and nails. He didn't want to hear about Kendrick anymore. He didn't want to think about Kendrick anymore. He wasn't in a relationship with Kendrick. Apparently his wife was.

He exhaled slowly, struggling with it all.

And he didn't struggle with emotions. He didn't... struggle.

But for her, he had. For her, he'd fought to be patient. Fought to be strong. Fought to understand. Fought to be the man she needed. And he'd believed she needed him. Not someone else, but *him*.

And he'd been wrong.

It was time to let her go. Time to let her return to the

city she loved, and the people she loved, and the work she loved.

It didn't mean he didn't love her.

It didn't mean he'd stop loving her.

It just meant he'd stop trying so hard. He'd stop giving her everything, and keeping nothing for himself. He'd stop making her number one. He'd stop making her the first thought every morning, and the last thought every evening.

It wouldn't be easy. Letting her go would be brutal. But trying to make it work, trying to believe in the impossible was breaking him. He was starting to feel broken.

*Lord, give me courage.*

*Give me strength.*

It was, finally, the beginning of the end.

BLAKE WAS IN her bedroom studying on the laptop when Tommy knocked on her door. It was midmorning and when he usually was out working with his grandfather.

She opened the door, waved him in. "Hi," she said, glad to see him, but also anxious.

It had been a tense good night the night before. She'd been waiting to see him today. Wanting to see him today. Wanting to be sure everything was okay... or as okay as it could be.

"I've got to get back outside," he said, staying in the doorway, instead of coming in. "Granddad has asked me to drive my uncle's truck to my cousin in Wyoming. With the weather warming up, he'd hoped I could get this done for him before I return to the circuit."

"When?" she asked, caught off guard.

"Today. This afternoon. Right after lunch."

"How far away is your cousin?"

"About five hours."

It was doable, she thought, mentally doing the math. "How would we get back?"

"We'd overnight tonight, and then on Saturday I'd fly to Bozeman, and you'd fly home to San Francisco."

"I thought I was here until Sunday."

"Billy's waiting for me. I've got to meet him in Texas. I've a lot of driving to do."

She couldn't speak. She shouldn't be shocked, but for some reason she hadn't expected this. Hadn't realized it was all ending so fast.

"It's just a day early," he added.

"So, I'd say goodbye to your mom and granddad here," she replied.

He nodded. "After lunch, yes."

"That's really soon."

"We'll want to arrive at the Sundowner before it's too late. Dot's invited us to dinner up at the big house, and I don't want to keep her waiting."

"Who is Dot?" Blake asked, feeling increasingly bewildered. "Is that your cousin's wife?"

"No. She owns the Sundowner Ranch. She's pretty amazing. I think you'll like her. And MerriBee is Cade's wife. I think you'll like her, too." He glanced at his watch. "I've got to get back to Granddad, but pack and be ready by noon. We'll eat and then be off."

# CHAPTER TEN

I T HAD BEEN a strangely emotional goodbye.

Blake didn't know what Tommy had told his mom, or his grandfather, but Melvin was somber as he gave her a hug, and Summer held on to Blake for an extra-long moment before letting her go. "You stay in touch," Summer said almost fiercely.

A lump filled Blake's throat. It was almost as if Summer knew she wasn't going to see her again. "I will," she answered. "Thank you for opening your home to me. Thank you for your wonderful hospitality. I am truly grateful—"

"Always here for you," Summer said, cutting her short, tears now in her eyes. "Remember that."

Blake swallowed hard, holding back her own emotion. "I will." And then she was waving goodbye and walking down the porch to the vintage truck in the driveway.

Tommy had already loaded the luggage so there was nothing else to do but get in the truck and go. Tommy climbed behind the steering wheel, started the engine, and they were off.

She leaned out the window and waved, and waved until

they disappeared from view. Blake settled back in her seat, adjusted her seat belt and fought tears.

Everything had changed. Tommy had pulled away. Tommy was ready to say goodbye—to her.

She felt it in her bones, felt it in her heart, and it was a terrible feeling. He'd always been her rock. Her safe place. And now he was done.

This was what she'd wanted, but still…

Still.

It wasn't until they reached the highway that Blake realized—once again—she hadn't taken a single photo. She should have taken pictures. At least one with Summer and Melvin.

At least one with Tommy.

She had none with Tommy, other than the photos taken the night of their wedding at the odd little chapel off the strip in Las Vegas, and she didn't even know where those pictures were. She didn't have them. She hadn't taken them home with her. Had he kept them?

"Remember our wedding?" she asked, glancing at him.

He lifted an eyebrow, and gave her a long look. "Of course."

"Someone took pictures of us that night, at the chapel."

"Yes."

"Do you have them?"

He nodded.

"Where are they?" she asked.

"In my trailer. In a safe deposit box." He glanced at her. "Do you want them?"

"You don't want them anymore?"

"There's no point, is there?"

"We can't still be friends?" she whispered.

"Sure, we can, but there's no need to keep wedding photos if we're friends."

She didn't know how to answer this, and anything she wanted to say was knotted with emotion, trapped in her chest.

For the next half hour Tommy just drove, and Blake sat next to him, trying not to think, or feel. The last thing she wanted to do was sit next to him and cry for five hours.

Tommy stopped for gas and cold drinks at a gas station outside of Billings. He handed her the bottle of water and slid behind the steering wheel. Once he was driving again, he started telling her about his cousin.

"Cade manages the Sundowner, one of the biggest family-owned ranches in the US. In summer, it's a dude ranch but the rest of the year it's a working cattle ranch. We'll overnight there, and tomorrow night, and then Saturday morning Cade will drop us off at the airport in Cody." Tommy glanced at her. "Have you ever been to Wyoming before?"

"No. I haven't been to Wyoming, or North or South Dakota, Idaho, or Nebraska. I think you know I pretty much haven't spent a lot of time outside of California and Arizona." She tried to smile. "Thanks to you I'm seeing more of America. And thanks to you, I'm discovering America is full of farms and ranches, small towns, medium-size cities, places where lots of really good people live."

"I think you'll like Cade. He's still getting to know us, just as we're still getting to know him, but I'm pretty comfortable with him. He reminds me of a brother more than a cousin."

"If he is your cousin, how is he new to the family?"

"He didn't know about us until recently. He's been looking for his missing sister, and a DNA test showed he was related to us. His dad, Samuel, was my dad's younger brother."

"The one your mom said was your dad's best friend?"

Tommy nodded. "Finding Cade is a big deal for Granddad. He had no idea that Samuel had a son, and Granddad had saved a lot of Samuel's things—clothes, pictures, trophies, this truck. Little by little, Granddad is handing it all over."

"I'd think Melvin would want to give Cade the truck himself."

"You'd think, but Granddad doesn't want to make this more emotional than it has to be."

"Does Cade know you're bringing him his dad's truck?"

Tommy shook his head.

"Oh, wow." She leaned back against the seat, ran a hand across the old dash. "How do you think Cade will react?"

"Like Granddad. A lot of bottled emotion." He paused. "He didn't have it so good growing up. His stepdad was abusive as all get out. His mom died when he was a senior in high school. All these years he felt alone. He felt as if he had no one, but now that we've found him—now that I've found him—not letting him go."

Tommy's words were particularly painful because she knew he was letting her go.

"I'm looking forward to meeting him," she said quietly.

"His wife, MerriBee, is a friend. I pointed her former house out to you during our walk in Marietta. It was the two-story Christmas house on Bramble."

"Oh, yes, I remember it." She bit her lower lip, trying to hide the tumultuous feelings rioting within her. "So, do they know I'm coming with you?"

"Yes."

"Have you said anything about me?"

"Just that I had a friend with me, and she'd need a room in the main house, if possible."

Blake glanced at him. "Where will you stay?"

"In Cade and MerriBee's cabin."

Her lips parted, but she made no sound. He just seemed more distant by the second.

As if reading her mind, he added, "They're not far apart. You're not being sent to Siberia."

"Who is in the main house?"

"Dot. Our hostess."

"So, Cade isn't the host?"

"He's going to inherit the Sundowner. On paper it's his, but as long as Dot is alive, it's her property, her heritage." He glanced at her again. "No reason to be nervous. I think you'll enjoy yourself. There's lots to do. You could do a guided ride, or go in one of the off-road vehicles to explore the ranch. And if there's snow, there's always the snow mobiles."

"I'm not really an outdoorsy adventure type," she said, forcing a smile. "But if there's a comfortable chair somewhere, I could always read."

"You'd love the Sundowner's library then. The living room always has a nice fire. It's a great house. One hundred years old, big vaulted ceilings with huge beams. Looks like one of those historic lodges you'd see in Yosemite or Yellowstone."

Her panic eased somewhat, but she was filled with regrets, and emotions she couldn't even deal with. Not yet. "I'm sorry I never got to meet Sophie and Joe."

"It's probably for the best. Sophie would have a hard time meeting you and letting you go. Better to not form more attachments than necessary. As it was, Mom took your departure pretty hard."

So Blake hadn't imagined Summer's tears. "I like your mom. I like your family."

The corner of his mouth pulled, but it wasn't a real smile. "I do, too."

❦

THEY REACHED THE Sundowner Ranch as the sun sank behind the mountains, painting the sky orange and red. Tommy navigated the steep approach to the ranch with ease. Lavender light spread across the ranch as he parked in front of an old log cabin.

"I'll let Cade know I'm here and then I'll drive you up to the house."

The front door opened even as he was turning the truck's engine off. A tall broad-shouldered cowboy that looked remarkably like Tommy's brother, Sam, stepped out, followed by a pretty redhead.

Tommy was out of the truck in a flash, hugging Cade, and then MerriBee. They were all talking and laughing and Blake climbed out more slowly, feeling forgotten. But then Tommy turned and came for her, walking her over to his cousin and his cousin's wife.

"Cade and MerriBee, this is my girl, Blake Eden. Or more formally known as Dr. Eden."

"Welcome," MerriBee said, giving Blake a swift hug. "That's a long drive from Paradise Valley. You must be feeling a little stiff."

"I'm good," Blake said, relaxing already. MerriBee was warm and kind, and Blake could use both right now.

Cade glanced over at the truck. "Nice set of wheels. What year?"

"It's a 1972."

"How does it run?"

"Like a dream." Tommy handed him the keys. "And it's yours."

Cade didn't take the keys. His gaze narrowed and he glanced at his wife, then back to Tommy. "What do you mean?"

"Granddad has been holding on to your dad's truck all these years. He says its time it came to you."

"I was just happy to get Dad's flannel shirt," Cade said lowly. "I can't—"

"It's yours, man. Granddad can't take care of it anymore. And if you want to sell it—"

"I don't," Cade interrupted.

Tommy shrugged. "Just saying, it's up to you. The pink slip is in the glove compartment. He's already signed it over to you."

Cade hugged Tommy and clapped his back, and when he stepped back, he looked overwhelmed by emotion.

Having spent the past five days with Melvin, Blake felt emotional, too.

MerriBee turned to Blake and gave her a smile. "How about I drive you up to the house, and get you settled while these guys clean up for dinner?"

THE MAIN HOUSE was just as Tommy had said—a huge sprawling, stunning example of park architecture, with a base of river rock, shingles, and massive logs. Passing through the front door, she saw the ceiling was vaulted, supported by big roughhewn beams. Blake glimpsed floor-to-ceiling windows in the dining room and the living room opposite. Both rooms were also anchored with huge stone fireplaces. Rich red wool carpets with Native American designs covered the stone and wood floor. A massive rustic, wrought iron chandelier hung in the entry, with an intricate iron and antler chandelier over the dining table.

Blake hadn't traveled a great deal, but she had been to Yosemite twice, and the Awahnee Hotel in the valley was probably her favorite hotel she'd ever stayed at, and this home was reminiscent of that—big, impressive, with soaring spaces and tall windows and French doors.

"Wow," she whispered, more to herself than anything, as MerriBee led the way up the staircase to the second floor. Framed artwork hung on the walls—art she recognized as some of America's greatest works.

Blake paused on the second floor landing, and leaned close to one huge canvas of the Rocky Mountains and read the signature. Bierstadt. *The* Bierstadt?

MerriBee turned, looked back at Blake, and seeing Blake's expression, nodded. "Yes." She pointed to other works on the walls of the second floor. "Remington, Russell, Seton."

MerriBee began walking again and Blake caught up as MerriBee opened a door halfway down the hall. "Dot's grandfather, Colonel Warner, knew many of the artists, financially supporting them, inviting them to stay here while they worked, or offering a rest during their travels. The colonel and Dot's father became collectors. Don't miss the Frederic Edwin Church in the dining room. Dot just got it back a few weeks ago. It had been on loan to the Metropolitan Museum of Art for the past two years."

"Amazing. I was going to ask if it's difficult leaving Marietta, but this place is incredible."

"Dot is incredible. I have so much love and respect for her. She's looking forward to meeting you at dinner." MerriBee glanced at her watch. "We eat at six. I'd say, six on the dot, but then it sounds like a play on words as Dot is very punctual."

"How formal is dinner?" Blake asked. "Jeans okay, or not?"

"You'll never see Dot in jeans at dinner, she always wears a skirt, but you'd be fine in jeans if your top half was a little bit dressy."

Alone in the bedroom, Blake glanced around, discovering she had her own private bathroom, as well as a big closet. The walls were paneled with a rich dark wood. The beams were stenciled with gold, red, and turquoise patterns. Her window was large and framed with floor-to-ceiling dark teal velvet curtains, the curtain edges fringed with gold, cream, and red tassels. Her room was as stunning as the rest of the house and going to the window, she looked out at the landscape shrouded in darkness. The mountains had disap-

peared, but she could see lights in the distance, and wondered if that's where Tommy was with Cade.

Her heart felt heavy and she put a hand to her chest,
holding the pain in.

She'd never doubted Tommy's love, never, until now.
But suddenly it seemed as if he'd unplugged from her, and
the idea of him taking his love back was crushing.

It was what she'd wanted to happen, it was what she'd
thought needed to happen, and yet, now that it was happening, it was also devastating.

It would be so much easier if she didn't love him so
much.

If she didn't need him so much.

Tears started in her eyes but she couldn't let it happen.
In the bathroom, she splashed cold water on her face,
shocking her, freezing the emotion. She couldn't fall apart,
not now, not before dinner. She was a guest here at Ms.
Warner's and she wasn't going to embarrass Tommy, or
herself.

TOMMY GOT THROUGH dinner with his usual smile, keeping
conversation flowing, knowing he had needed to be a good
guest. He'd become quite fond of Dorothy Warner since
meeting her last year, and was genuinely glad to see her
again, and hear what she had to say about current events, as
well as the future of the cattle ranching industry. Cade had

warned him before dinner that Dot had a fall a few weeks ago and her wrist was in a cast, but she didn't mention it, and he didn't ask.

Dot was quite taken with Blake, which didn't surprise him. Blake was beautiful, brilliant, articulate. He could hardly take his eyes off of her, even though it was bittersweet watching her talk with Dot, her slim body leaning forward, her hands gesturing with her passionate answers. Her white blouse was rolled up at the sleeves revealing thick gold bangles on both wrists. Gold hoops were at her ears. She looked gorgeous, like a model, her curls pulled back, her high elegant cheekbones gleaming with just a shimmer of highlighter, her full lips a lush red.

He'd spent three years waiting for her, believing in them, believing that his faith wasn't misplaced.

He'd been wrong.

He didn't blame her. She'd told him right away they'd made a mistake, but he hadn't wanted to believe it. The fact that she wanted out only made him more determined to win her heart. He was that competitive. And maybe that egotistical. He truly believed if he just tried hard enough—he'd succeed at whatever he set his mind to. Until now, he'd been successful. Tommy Wyatt rarely lost. Tommy rarely failed. Tommy only knew how to win.

When he was seven, a mare had died giving birth in the Wyatt barn. Tommy had been there with his brothers, trying to help Granddad save the mare, and then the foal. The foal was suffering, struggling, and one by one the others left when the foal was clearly not going to make it. Tommy never left. He spent the night holding the foal. He was still there in the morning when his mom and grandfather returned to the barn at dawn. The foal was still alive, too. Tommy patiently, persistently got the foal to drink a little milk from the bottle Granddad had created for occasions like this one.

That foal grew up to be Tommy's stallion—a horse that followed Tommy everywhere, a horse that became his first horse to compete in the junior rodeos with him.

The horse he learned to win on.

The horse that taught him loyalty and patience was more important than being right.

His eyes burned as he looked at Blake across the table and knowing he was losing her was every bit as painful as that night when he was seven and told the foal would die, that it had been too badly injured in birth to survive.

Tommy wanted to prove the world wrong.

He wanted to prove Blake wrong.

But she was a woman, a smart, competent woman who needed to do what was best for her, even if it broke his heart.

She was breaking his heart.

He pressed his lips together, a thin hard line, holding the emotion in, even as he tried to take it all in—her, the glory of her, the smile and radiance, the elegance and brilliance.

Suddenly, her head turned and she looked at him for a

long, timeless moment. Their gaze locked, held, and he knew that even though she would be leaving soon, she did love him. Their love had been real. Unfortunately, there were just circumstances working against them. Perhaps if they'd met when he was older and retired, perhaps if she'd been practicing medicine for a while, they'd be able to see a way clear. As it was, they just wanted—needed—different things.

He didn't blame her. He respected her. But he couldn't remain close to her, not any longer. It just made the separation harder.

When Dot signaled dinner was over, Cade and MerriBee indicated they'd clear the table to help the kitchen staff, but Blake said she'd be happy to do it. Tommy immediately offered to help her but MerriBee shook her head. "Why don't Blake and I just handle it, and that way you boys can catch up some more, and Blake and I can talk? I'm dying to get to know her better."

Dot seemed to approve, saying she wanted to ask Tommy some questions about management of the Wyatt ranch, and so Tommy and Cade walked Dot to the living room while MerriBee and Blake cleared the table and then once the dishes were all in the kitchen, MerriBee made both of them cups of herbal tea and they carried them to the library where they could visit alone.

"So, tell me everything," MerriBee said, getting comfortable in one of the wingchairs flanking the massive stone fireplace. "How did you two meet?"

Blake settled in her chair, grateful this was an easy question. "He saved me from some drunk guys that wouldn't leave me alone."

"How many were there? Drunk guys?"

"Four." Blake grimaced. "They were persistent. Wouldn't take no."

"Tommy's fists did a little talking?"

Blake laughed. "Does everyone know him so well?"

"He's a Wyatt, and I've known the Wyatts for years. They're tough. They don't mess around. They're also loyal and honest. Straightforward. Which I appreciate, seeing as I've married into the family."

"No regrets becoming part of the family?"

"Absolutely none. I'm happier than I've ever been."

Blake couldn't find her voice for a long moment. Merri-Bee's happiness was evident. Tangible. She radiated warmth. Hope. When she smiled, it was like being bathed in sunshine. MerriBee glowed with love and life, and something else. Conviction? Purpose?

"I understand we have something else in common," Blake said. "You're a nurse?"

"Yes."

"Tommy said you're in hospice."

"Yes."

"What makes you so strong?" Blake asked.

MerriBee shook her head. "I'm not strong."

"You moved here from Marietta, live in the middle of

nowhere, you practice an area of medicine that is so hard—"

"I love what I do."

Blake put a hand to her chest. "I love what I do, but I'm trying to heal and save people. You can't save anyone."

"I make them comfortable on their way out. It's every bit as important as the labor and delivery nurses, welcoming babies into the world, into life."

Blake's eyes stung. She thought of her future and what awaited her, and felt immense gratitude that there were people like MerriBee who felt as they did. "You're amazing."

"I'm not. It's just my mission, my gift. We all have one."

"I don't think I have one," Blake confessed. "Other than a determination to take care of others."

"There's your mission."

"Yes, but it doesn't feel very organic, not after hearing you tell me about yours."

"Oh, mine wasn't organic. I didn't start out in hospice. I started out as a labor and delivery nurse, and then was rotated to another floor during a staffing shortage, ending up on the oncology ward." MerriBee sat in silence a moment before continuing. "It was while I was working in oncology at the hospital I ended up taking care of my old boyfriend."

"He had cancer?" Blake asked, astonished.

MerriBee nodded. "I never understood why we broke up. John didn't give me an explanation. He just disappeared. He was an incredible athlete, a member of the Olympic ski team, and I tried to move on as much as I could, but I felt like a failure. I felt as if I'd failed him. Then one day at Marietta Medical, I entered a room and there he was. On my floor. In my care."

"Was his cancer advanced?"

Again MerriBee nodded. She stopped talking, her gaze unfocused, somewhere else.

Blake's heart raced. She was stunned. "He'd never told you?"

"No." MerriBee set her teacup on the table next to her, folded her hands. "I was in shock. I couldn't believe what I was seeing, and then later, I refused to accept that he wasn't going to remain on earth long." Her lips curved, expression rueful. "Something to know about me—I'm stubborn. Really stubborn. And I loved him. Just adored him. John was one of the most wonderful, positive, selfless people I'd ever known, and even ill, he was inspiring. He, and his faith, inspired me.

"I just couldn't let him go, not without a fight. I spent every hour I could, when not working, with him. I don't know what it was, the fact that he wasn't alone, or the power of love, but John began to eat again, and he handled his meds better, and he went into remission—when no one expected it. We married, bought a house, and had almost a year together. And then he died."

Again, silence stretched. MerriBee's smile was gentle, thoughtful. "I consider myself fortunate that I was there with him in his final weeks. I made sure he knew he was loved, and that he was as comfortable as he could be. I played his favorite music, our favorite songs, and we talked. When he couldn't talk anymore, I told him how lucky we'd been to find each other again, and reminded him of all the wonderful things we had done together. Every day I just loved him, and then he was gone. It was a peaceful end."

"You had peace?" Blake asked.

"I had peace that he hadn't been alone through that. I was grateful we'd bought him more time… that we'd bought us more time. That meant everything to me."

"No regrets?"

"No. He still lives in my heart." MerriBee looked down at her left hand, gently adjusted her wedding ring. "What hospice care has taught me is that when we love people, really love them, they might be physically gone, but they're not gone. Cade knows this. Cade respects the relationship I'd had with John. He has never felt threatened, or said he felt like he was second fiddle. Before Cade, I was a different person, and I'm grateful for my life with John, and now I'm grateful, so grateful, for my life with Cade."

"You know how you said, it seemed like the cancer went into remission? And then the cancer came back?" Blake asked.

"Yes."

"How much time was there between it returning, and him dying?"

"It had always been there. It had just stopped… progressing."

"And when it started progressing again?"

"It returned with a vengeance." MerriBee's voice cracked. "It took him quickly."

There was so much pressure on Blake's chest, in her throat. It was hard to speak. "Did you expect that?"

"We both knew it was a possibility." She hesitated. "More than a possibility. An eventuality. We knew he'd never be cured. There was no cure at that point, not when it had metastasized as it had. What we were doing was buying time."

"It seems terrible. Painful."

MerriBee wiped a tear from the corner of her eye. Her voice dropped. "In some ways it was freeing. Because when you realize you don't have forever, you kind of grow up. You decide it's time to let go of the petty stuff. Since you don't have forever, you choose to love. Knowing time is finite, you just open your heart and love. And isn't that what we all want? Unconditional love? Love that is supportive, compassionate, kind?"

Her eyes filled with tears and MerriBee passed a hand over her eyes, clearing the tears. "John was really young. Not even thirty. And I never wanted to be a widow. It wasn't a distinction I looked for, but on the other hand, I very much wanted to be his wife. I wanted to be a family with him. I wanted us to have that. It was probably more important to me than it was to him. He didn't want me to hurt. He didn't want me to grieve, but I would have hurt either way."

"You never had children in your marriage."

"No children. He wasn't—" She broke off, shook her head. "It wasn't an option."

Blake was overwhelmed by emotions, overwhelmed by the similarity between John's story and her own. "Do you and Cade want kids?"

"Yes, but we're waiting. Just a little bit. We want to enjoy each other. We want to just be a family together and then maybe in a couple of years."

"Your definition of family doesn't have to include kids?"

"Children are one aspect of a family. John and I marrying, buying a house together, living together, having our special Christmas together, that was family for us. And even if the time was short, it was very satisfying. It was everything."

UPSTAIRS IN HER bed with the handsome antique frame, Blake couldn't sleep, overwhelmed by everything that had happened that day.

Goodbye to Summer and Melvin.

Meeting Cade and MerriBee.

Dinner with Dot.

The house, the history, the huge ranch run by a woman when women didn't get much respect, never mind, rule the West. But Dot had, and did.

Blake couldn't stop thinking about MerriBee's first husband, who died young of cancer and how MerriBee had been there with him until the end.

It was what Blake wanted for herself, but wasn't sure she deserved. Her cancer had taken over so many people's lives, had changed her parents' marriage, had made them anxious for her. Overprotective as well. Every blood test, every doctor's visit was stressful and the waiting for results, intense. Would the cancer be growing again? Would the end be near? Would they be able to fight again, or would they be making decisions on how to keep her comfortable?

These questions were always in the back of her mind.

These questions had helped her keep her distance from Tommy.

This week was everything she would have wanted if there had been no cancer. This week, this life, would have been it.

The wife of Tommy Wyatt, champion cowboy.

Her eyes watered and stung and she put her arm over her eyes, the lump in her throat making it hard to breathe.

She'd be leaving here in just over twenty-four hours. She'd get on her jet plane and fly away, leaving her husband and heart.

She was so tempted to tell him everything, so tempted to explain it all but that wasn't fair. She was playing the desperation card, positioning herself as a victim, and that wasn't how she wanted to have him. She wouldn't trap him. She wouldn't have him pity her. She wanted his love, but not like this. Not when he'd finally decided he was ready to move on.

With so many thoughts, so many emotions, it was no wonder she couldn't fall asleep and stay asleep, and it was only after four when she finally dozed off, and slept at all.

TOMMY DIDN'T SLEEP.

It had been a long, long night, and he left bed at four when he heard Cade moving around in the cabin. Cade was an early riser and so Tommy dressed and met his cousin in the kitchen. They had a cup of coffee together before grabbing hats and coats and heading to the barn to saddle horses for a morning ride.

They'd ridden up to the top of the ridge in semidarkness, reaching the peak in time to see the sun rise. Tommy's jaw worked as the sky lightened, and the sun rose gold, casting long bright rays of light across the foothills and valley below. Amazing how the sun rose every morning despite all the human struggles. Amazing how beautiful the world was even when you hurt. Maybe suffering made nature even more beautiful.

He hurt. But he'd survive it. He'd spent most of his life getting thrown, hit, bruised, broken and he was still here. Tough. Stronger than before.

He glanced at Cade and saw that his cousin was watching him, his gaze narrowed beneath the brim of his Stetson.

"I've never seen you like this," Cade said.

"Like this?"

"No smile. No jokes. No laughter." Cade studied him a moment. "Want to talk about it?"

Tommy shook his head. "No." And then he looked out at the horizon and the gilded valley, glowing beneath the rising sun. "Maybe."

Cade's horse shifted, but otherwise he just waited.

Tommy gathered his thoughts, heart so heavy. "I married the girl of my dreams, and it's over. I didn't think it'd end this way." He made a rough sound deep in his chest. "I didn't think it'd end."

AFTER BREAKFAST ON her own in the huge dining room, Blake was restlessly pacing the living room and hallways, trying to ease her panic and anxiety.

She was exhausted.

Her head ached. Her eyes were dry and gritty. Her stomach churned and she wasn't sure she could even keep the one poached egg down.

She felt in desperate need of a confidant, someone who could help her, advise her. In the past, she talked to Kendrick, but Kendrick wasn't the right person now.

Kendrick would never be the right person again.

MerriBee walked through the front door just then, a basket of freshly cut daffodils on her arm. Relief washed through Blake. "Can I talk to you?" she said to MerriBee. "Can I trust you?"

MerriBee's eyebrow arched. "Provided you're not going to tell me that you robbed a string of banks in Wyoming or Montana."

Blake smiled. "No robberies, no violence, nothing illegal."

MerriBee gestured Blake to follow her, and they went to the butler's pantry off the main kitchen, adjacent to the dining room. MerriBee reached into the cabinet for a vase, using the small sink to fill the vase with water.

Blake watched MerriBee put the daffodils in the vase, arranging them.

Could she trust MerriBee? Her gut said yes. Her gut said MerriBee had integrity. "Tommy and I are married." She blurted the words, and held her breath a moment, and then hurried on. "We married in Las Vegas over three years ago, after a chance meeting while he was at the NFRs. It was a rather spectacular first meet, and I fell for him, hard. I don't just fall in love, either. I'm not a romantic. I'm not the fizzy, dreamy, wishful sort."

MerriBee pushed the vase back and faced Blake.

Blake's gaze met MerriBee's and after a moment Blake continued, "I'm practical, a realist... rational. But three days after Tommy and I met, we got married, going to a chapel off the strip Saturday night following the NFR awards ceremony. Sunday, I returned to San Francisco. He went home to Montana to be with his family for Christmas." She held her breath, counted to five. "We didn't see each other until a week ago when I showed up at his rodeo in Salinas."

Blake waited, giving MerriBee a chance to speak, but MerriBee remained silent.

"This week I came to Montana with Tommy, not to make things work," Blake added, "but to get his signature on the divorce petition. It was part of the deal I'd made with him. I'd spend the week with him, and then he'd sign the papers. So here I am." She tried to smile, but couldn't. "Tomorrow, I return to San Francisco, and it will be over. But now, after almost a week together, I'm not sure I want us to be over. But Tommy is tired of my indecision, and it's hurt him. He's the one who decided no more. He is right, by the way. He's made the right decision. But it's killing me."

MerriBee pulled out one of the short stools beneath the counter and sat down. "Wow. I didn't see any of that coming." She reached over to the vase and broke off a wilted flower. "And none of the Wyatts know?"

Blake shook her head.

"That explains why he hasn't been interested in any of the women I introduced him to. Tom's been a monk. A saint."

"He's a really good person. I'm crazy about him," Blake admitted. "The last thing I wanted to do was hurt him, but I have. It just wasn't going to work with us, though, not with our careers. One of us would have to move, and neither of us can."

MerriBee held the wilted flower. "You are in your last

few months of residency. I would think you have the most flexibility."

"It sounds like that, but I don't want to leave my parents. It's been a hard ride—" Blake made a face. "Now I sound like I'm all rodeo lingo. But things haven't been easy for them, and if I move across the country, they will worry about me. I don't want them worried about me."

"Won't they worry about you even if you're down the street? Not sure how distance changes parental concern."

"When your John left the hospital, and you two lived together in the same house, did you worry less about him? Did you feel better seeing him, and being there so you could take care of him?"

"Yes, but that's an entirely different circumstance. He was ill—" MerriBee broke off, her eyes narrowing, expression firming.

For a long moment there was just silence.

For the first time, it was quiet enough to hear the ticking of the grandfather clock in the great hallway.

"Do you... are you... ill?"

"I have ovarian cancer. I'm holding steady but not in remission."

"Tommy doesn't know," MerriBee said, "does he?"

Blake shook her head.

"He loves you, Blake."

"I love him, which is why he can't know. It would change everything... it would change him, and I don't want that. Tommy deserves everything, and if he stuck with me, he'd end up with nothing." Her voice broke. "So, no, he's not going to know."

"You think it's better for you to leave and divorce him, and let him think it's because he's not good enough? That he's not valuable enough?"

"Yes." Blake exhaled hard, eyes stinging. "Because he might be hurt for a little bit, but once the door is closed, truly closed, Tommy will move on, just like you moved on. You found Cade, and he's perfect for you. You are both so happy. Once I'm out of the picture, Tommy will have that. He'll find his forever person. I know it in my heart."

MerriBee rose from the stool and walked to the dining room doorway, facing away from Blake. "I think you're wrong to keep the truth from him. I think you don't understand the nature of love. Love isn't fearful. It's brave. It believes all things." She turned, looked at Blake. "It will devastate him to find out the truth later. And he will find out the truth. It's not something you can keep a secret forever."

"But hopefully by the time he discovers the truth, he'll be married and starting a family, and he'll be grateful, MerriBee. He'll be grateful I didn't waste the next five years of his life, when he could be making love and making babies. If he stays with me, it's only going to get worse. It will never get better."

"I loved being there for John."

"It also caused you unspeakable pain."

MerriBee's eyes slowly filled with tears. "It would have been worse for me to think he'd die alone."

"I have my parents. They will be with me."

MerriBee clasped her hands into fists. "You do Tommy a terrible injustice."

"I'm trying to protect him, and that is justice."

MerriBee wiped away a tear and walked out through the dining room, leaving Blake in the butler's pantry with the daffodils and glass-fronted cabinets filled with gleaming china and glittering crystal.

The small room was warm and yet Blake felt chilled.

None of this was going as planned. She'd thought she'd feel calm, even heroic, making these decisions, but instead she felt lost.

Defeated.

Was she making a mistake?

Should she tell Tommy the truth?

No.

No. She wouldn't. She couldn't. She needed to keep what was left of her control and dignity.

# CHAPTER ELEVEN

TOMMY WAS WAITING for her after lunch. "Feel like going for a walk?" he asked.

Blake nodded, conscious that she looked as exhausted as she felt. She followed him out through one of the side doors, around to a walled garden with its tidy dormant rose beds. Despite the brightness of the sun and the vivid blue sky, the garden's bleakness depressed Blake. It just looked barren.

Like her.

No womb, no ovaries, no eggs, no babies.

She'd always wanted children. As an only child, she'd been desperate for brothers and sisters and had vowed to one day have a big family, five, six, seven kids, she told her parents once. She'd have so many her parents wouldn't even be able to remember all their names.

She'd once been so fierce. As a girl, she'd given her parents such a hard time. From the very start, she'd been precocious, reading early, learning math early, fascinated by all things growing and living. She'd loved biology, loved science, loved bodies and human anatomy. She hadn't wanted to become a doctor, not initially. She'd wanted to be a scientist, wanted to discover something significant, something that would heal people, something that would make a difference in the world, and then she started feeling off in high school. She was losing weight, and feeling weak, but she thought maybe she was doing too much, and dropped off the track team. She stopped playing tennis, but she kept losing weight. Her back hurt and her pelvis hurt and she was tired all the time. It was just bad cramps, typical of being a teenager. Even her mother said the same thing until she accidentally walked into Blake's bedroom one day while Blake was changing.

Her mom knew right away something was very wrong. Blake was all skin and bones, except for her abdomen which was quite swollen.

No one could believe the diagnosis when it came later that week. Blake was just fifteen. Fifteen-year-old girls didn't get ovarian cancer.

Not unless they had *X*.

Which she had.

Tommy had sat down at a table beneath the weathered trellis. In summer, the trellis would be beautiful, covered in roses, but now it was just bare stalks with thorns. Blake lightly touched one of the thorns and then sat down, too. It was obvious he had something to say. She dreaded it, whatever it was.

Fortunately, he didn't keep her waiting. He pulled out papers from inside his leather coat pocket and placed them on the table between them. "I was researching the difference between filing for divorce in California and Montana, and we'd do better filing in Montana. It's much simpler, and faster."

She pressed her knuckles to her chair.

"Montana has a no-fault divorce law," he said. "To get a divorce in Montana, the court must decide if we have lived apart for more than 180 days before the petition for divorce is filed—which we have."

She nodded.

"Since that's the case," he added, "our marriage will be dissolved quickly."

"How quickly?" she asked.

"If it's an uncontested divorce, which it will be, and we qualify for joint summary dissolution, which we do, we'll be free in twenty days."

"Can you explain what an uncontested divorce would be in Montana?"

"Since we have no shared property, or children, we just need to agree on support, and if we both agree, we're done. Neither of us will contest the divorce."

"Support?" she repeated. "Financial support?"

He nodded.

"No." Blake half-rose, shook her head. "I'm not asking, or taking, money from you. I don't want your money—"

"You're my wife."

She laughed, blinked. "That you're divorcing."

"It's what you wanted. It's why you came to see me in Salinas." He put his hand over hers. "Please, sit. Let's not make this more uncomfortable than it is. I want to make sure you are taken care of, and cutting you a check is what I want to do."

She looked at him, searching his face, trying to see what was behind the cool blue gaze because he'd disappeared, shuttered his eyes, shuttered his heart, removed himself from her. It was awful. It was like being kicked from a warm car into an icy tundra. She was in shock and couldn't find her bearings. "I don't need money," she said lowly. *I just needed you.*

*I will always just want you.*

"San Francisco is expensive," he continued, as if she hadn't spoken. "You should have enough to buy your own home, in a good neighborhood, a place large enough you could eventually have your parents come live with you, should you want."

She closed her eyes, held her breath, trying to block his words out.

Everything was becoming so hard, so final.

"I can set you up with an investment account, so the money will earn until you know what you want to do—"

"No." She opened her eyes, the lump in her throat huge, painful, just like the pain in her heart. "I'll only agree to the uncontested divorce if there's no money involved. I have never wanted, or needed, you to support me financially. I fell for you. Not your bank account."

His gaze clashed with hers but she wouldn't look away. It might make him feel better to send her away with some money but it would only make her feel worse. And she didn't need to feel worse.

"We can do this all online," he said. "I've printed everything off, though, so we can discuss it first. If everything makes sense, and looks good, we can finish the rest in the house, either on your laptop or mine."

She brought the paperwork close to her, and read through the pages, reading slowly, carefully, until she reached the end, and then after the slightest hesitation nodded. "Looks fine."

He rose. "Alright, let's do this then."

She followed him into the house, aware that this was her fault. She'd done this to him, to them. But it was too late now to change her mind. She couldn't toy with Tommy's emotions like that. And in the end, this was for the best, it really was.

But right now, in that moment where she felt so raw, it was hard to believe it was the truth.

SOMEHOW AFTER COMPLETING the online application, they were able to rejoin everyone else for pre-dinner cocktails, another Sundowner tradition. Blake wasn't sure how she'd manage a cocktail gathering when she felt so low, but Dot had invited another couple for drinks and dinner. The beautiful brunette was a country singer, one Blake had heard on the radio many times. Ashley Bragg, and her husband, Nash, had just arrived that day and would be staying in one of the big summer cabins for the next month.

Ashley was writing new music and wanted quiet and having spent time at the Sundowner as a girl, always liked to return when in need of rest and inspiration. Her handsome husband, twenty-seven-year-old Nash, had grown up on an Oklahoma ranch and was looking forward to having time in the saddle, and assisting Cade and the hired hands, basically doing whatever man's work needed to be done.

"After seven months of nonstop touring, and being a glorified roadie, I need to escape busses and jets and traffic and noise," Nash said, raising his beer. "Thank you for having us. This is a slice of heaven, Miss Warner."

Ashley agreed. "Thank you. You know how much I love coming back each time. I do my best writing here, too."

With Ashley and Nash at dinner, conversation flowed easily, with Ashley and Nash entertaining everyone with their stories of life on the road, and how performing at the Grand Ole Opry was still Ashley's favorite thing she'd ever done.

As it turned out, Ashley had met Tommy several years ago when Ashley performed at the Houston rodeo. She hadn't been married yet and she'd flirted with Tommy, but Tommy hadn't flirted back. "I wondered if I'd lost my charm," she said, dimpling as she smiled, "but then Tommy introduced me to his brother Billy, and he took me to dinner later that night, was a real gentleman."

"Now you're making me jealous, sugar," Nash said, stroking the back of Ashley's long dark hair, but he didn't sound or look jealous at all. If anything, he seemed blissfully content.

Ashley gave him a teasing smile before looking at Blake. "Now I know why he wasn't interested in me. He had you." She raised her wineglass in a toast. "To honorable men, and I do believe we have three sitting at this table."

Blake smiled and sipped her wine, but on the inside she was numb, almost dead. She didn't dislike Ashley but everything about this dinner was painful. Miserable. Blake was grateful when dinner was finally over and Dot was inviting everyone to the living room for after-dinner liqueurs and coffees.

Blake began to clear the table but tonight Dot had extra staff and they shooed her out of the dining room.

She hesitated outside the living room, not wanting to go in and listen to more of the Ashley and Nash show. Maybe she was being petty, but it was hard to listen to newlyweds gush when she felt so terrible.

MerriBee approached Blake in the hall. "You okay?"

"I have a headache," Blake said.

"Let me get some painkillers from the medicine cabinet," MerriBee said. "Unless you have some?"

"I do. They're in my room."

"I'll walk you up," MerriBee said.

"That's not necessary," Blake answered, on the verge of tears.

MerriBee glanced to the living room and then back at Blake. "I wanted to talk to you about something, if you don't mind."

"Of course not."

They went upstairs to Blake's guest room. Blake shook out three tablets from the pill case in her vanity bag, and washed them down with the bottle of water on her bedside table.

MerriBee sat down on the edge of Blake's bed and patted the mattress. "Come sit with me."

The last thing Blake wanted was to talk. She craved solitude. She craved a dark room and a pillow to stifle the sound of her crying. But MerriBee was such a kind person that Blake didn't have the heart to ask her to leave.

It took MerriBee a moment to speak. She looked almost uncomfortable as she chose her words. "I saw paperwork earlier. Did you and Tommy sign it?"

"We did it all online this afternoon."

"So it's done?" MerriBee asked.

Blake nodded once.

For a long moment, there was just silence as MerriBee digested the news. Blake tried to ignore how tender she felt on the inside. It would be so easy to just break... to fall apart... but she didn't want to do that, couldn't do that, not here, not in front of Tommy's family.

"Cade is concerned about Tommy," MerriBee said after a moment. "They went on a morning ride, and Tommy asked Cade to pray with him. To give him strength." Merri-Bee's voice grew husky. "You look equally miserable. Are you certain this is the right thing to do?"

"We've already hit send." Blake tried to smile but couldn't.

"Divorces take time."

"Twenty business days in our case."

"And you're okay with this?"

"I love Tommy. How could I not? He's… everything. He's amazing. He's a world champion. The best of the best."

"The best of the best," MerriBee repeated. "And you're letting him go?"

"I don't deserve him. I don't deserve his patience, his kindness, his faith in me. I'm not good for him. I haven't been—" Her eyes burned and she blinked. She tried hard to keep the tears back. "I'm driven and ambitious but some-times I don't even know why I'm so driven and ambitious. Sometimes I wonder what it's for? Who am I doing this for? For me? My parents? Society? Am I driven because I need approval? Because it set me apart when I was a little girl, and teachers responded to it?"

Blake fell silent, struggling to compose herself. "From the beginning, Tommy has liked me and seen me, appreciating that I am this smart, ambitious woman. And he had no problem with it. Which is why Tommy deserves someone better. He deserves someone who will put him first."

"Don't you think that's up to him? Are you going to juvenilize him by making decisions for him? Or about what's best for him? That, in my opinion, isn't fair."

Blake didn't say anything. She felt exhausted and confused and her head was pounding so hard now she felt like throwing up.

"Do you know what makes Tommy so good at his job?" MerriBee asked gently.

Blake shook her head.

"Tommy is tough. He is the youngest of four tough boys, raised by his tough granddad after his dad died when he was maybe two years old. His mom has health issues and she struggles to get around. And you know what? Tommy never misses her birthday, he never misses his granddad's birthday, he has never missed anything important for any of his brothers. When it's a niece or nephew's birthday, he is there. I knew Tommy before I'd ever met my husband. Tommy is generous and giving. He helped me with the delivery of my Christmas baskets when a storm hit, and I couldn't get them all delivered in Marietta. And then when his family didn't know how to react to Cade, Tommy drove to Wyoming in practically blizzard conditions to make sure Cade knew he was wanted and welcome."

MerriBee's voice dropped. "If you've noticed, Tommy doesn't ask for anything for himself. He never has, and he never will. So, you're either going to love him for him, and you're going to want to be there for him, or you're not. That's the real question and the challenge. This isn't about cancer. This isn't about hiding the truth from him. It's about being his best friend, being his partner and confidant, someone he can talk to and lean on. And if you're not that person, then yes, let him go. Tommy won't always be a rodeo cowboy. He'll get off the circuit and want to be a family man. Every Wyatt has wanted that. So can you be a family with him? Don't look down the road. Don't look at the amount of time you have, or don't have. Just focus on the life you want. The life he wants. Can you have that together? Those are the real questions you should be asking. John never let me answer those for myself. Don't try to answer them for Tommy."

"I don't want to cut him loose."

"But you're not sure—"

"I will die," Blake said, voice rough. "And it will hurt him."

"It will," MerriBee agreed. "But don't think you're not hurting him now."

BLAKE NEVER MADE it back downstairs that evening. She sent word with MerriBee that she wasn't feeling well, and was calling it a night.

Blake drank more water, took a bath, put a cold washcloth across her face to hide how swollen her eyes were from crying, and then climbed into bed.

Even though she hadn't slept well the night before, she couldn't relax and sleep now.

She'd worried about making love this week, worried that he—or she—would want to, but she knew in her heart it was the one thing they couldn't do.

She couldn't get that close, and then walk away, let him go. Being in his arms was her favorite place to be. Being his, made her complete.

She wasn't the most experienced woman. Because of her cancer, she'd never dated in high school, not seriously. There had been boys she'd liked, one in particular, but they'd just started going out when she was diagnosed and he was scared of her cancer, scared of how sick she looked going through chemo. She understood his unease. She had a hard time liking herself bald, liking herself ill. It was hard to be attracted to someone who looked alien… and had… issues.

Tommy had been her first real love, her only true love. And maybe if there hadn't been Tommy, she could have fallen in love with Kendrick, but there was Tommy. That was the inescapable truth. There was Tommy.

And then there was her cancer, which couldn't be cured. It was too late for that. And so she was torn, did she look at the big picture, or did she focus on the present?

Focusing on the present meant she could be happy now, but by being happy now, it would make Tommy unhappy later, and that wasn't right, or fair.

All of these thoughts had been going through her head all week. Now the thoughts were amplified. Tomorrow everything changed again.

A knock on her door at eleven got her out of bed. She went to the door, opened it, knowing it was Tommy. She was right.

"Can I come in?" he asked.

She opened the door wider, let him enter, and then quietly closed it behind him.

"Did I wake you up?" he asked.

"I can't sleep," she said.

"Me, either."

He sat down on the edge of her bed, hands hanging between his knees. He looked bad. Beat.

She went to him, put a hand on his shoulder, and then touched his head, easing her palm over the back of his head. She did her best to soothe him and yet it wasn't enough. She could feel his pain and sadness, but at the same time, she knew he hadn't changed his mind.

She hadn't changed hers, either.

"Want to stay with me tonight?" she whispered.

"It'll make it worse tomorrow," he said.

"I know. But at least tonight we'd feel better."

"I'd like to feel better."

Her chest ached and her heart felt as if it had tumbled somewhere near her feet. "Me, too."

"Then I stay." Tommy eased off one boot, and then the other. She watched him take off his shirt, and then the T-shirt underneath, and then finally his jeans.

He climbed into bed in just his boxers and she crawled into bed next to him and was so glad when his arms went around her.

For a long time they just lay entwined, his arms around her, and her holding him. They didn't talk. She almost didn't breathe and then somewhere down the hall a clock chimed midnight. Morning would be here before they knew it.

She sighed, already heartbroken, and then she didn't know if she turned to him or he turned to her, but his mouth covered hers and there was no going back.

She wasn't sure if that was why Tommy came to her room at the Sundowner, but it didn't matter. He was here and she wanted him, all of him. She wanted every minute with him. She wanted all the things she wouldn't have later. And as their kiss deepened, she kissed him fiercely, passionately, giving him everything, and all of her.

Maybe this was supposed to happen.

Maybe love wasn't something you could stop, maybe love didn't end.

Maybe it had been inevitable from the beginning that they would be here tonight, him above her, in her, completing her. They made love twice during the night, and she was still in his arms when the morning sun pierced her window, finding space between the curtains which had been partially drawn. She opened her eyes, looked at Tommy, who still slept. His eyelashes were so long. They rested on his high cheekbones. He looked strangely vulnerable. Not young, just exposed, open, and it crossed her mind that he was not as tough as the persona shared with the world.

It crossed her mind that perhaps, despite his family, despite his career and fans, he was actually quite alone.

Because if he had waited for her all these years, if he had hoped to reconcile with her, it would have been a difficult secret to keep, hiding his love, biding his time. Three years of biding his time.

She leaned over and gently kissed his lips. He stirred, his arm tightening around her, his hand pressed against her backside.

"Good morning," he said, voice rough and raspy.

She put her cheek on his hard chest. "Good morning."

"It's Saturday," he said.

"I know."

HE HADN'T SLEPT much the night before.

It was hard to sleep after making love to your wife, the keeper of your heart, the one you were letting go in the morning.

He was letting go of her, too. He couldn't hang on any longer. There was no point in hanging on. He didn't doubt her love, but he also understood that she wasn't meant to live the life he lived. He finally understood that their goals and dreams were incompatible. It wasn't that being a doctor in a big city meant more to her than he did, it was just that before she'd ever met him, she knew who she was, she knew what she needed to do, and he wasn't going to come between her and her mission. He wasn't going to try to convince her that they can make it together, because she was right. He was being impractical. It would create so much stress on both of them if they tried to go back and forth, juggle their lives and commitments, juggle their families, squeezing their love into a few days here and there each month.

It wasn't what he wanted for himself either.

If he was completely honest, he wanted more. He didn't want a part-time wife. He didn't want a part-time love. He wanted to wake with his wife and go to bed with his wife and spend most of his life with her, not away from her, not waiting for her. If that was selfish, then he was going to be selfish.

He loved her enough to let her go, let her find happiness with someone who would live in the city with her, who would work at a hospital near her, who would talk to her about her work, and understood her cases and patients. Tommy could listen to her, but he'd never be a doctor, he'd never truly understand what she went through. Fate was a strange thing. So was destiny. It was fate that they met, but destiny tore them apart.

Tommy didn't want to leave bed, but soon he'd have to, and then the day would begin and the changes would happen. It was both awful and a relief. The goodbye would happen later this morning, and then finally, it would be done.

Over.

Once he put her on the plane, there would be no more thoughts of her, no more longing for her, or waiting patiently, and impatiently, for her. If there was something he was good at, it was closing a door. It was why he'd never closed the door before. He'd kept it open, for her, and only her. Only now it was time for them both to move on, and he saw that now. He felt it. Accepted it. This wasn't the ending he'd wanted, but sometimes you didn't get what you wanted. Sometimes you just had to suck it up.

At least his family didn't know all the details. As it was, his mom would miss Blake. His mom, who took forever to warm up, had taken quickly to Blake. It was almost as if Blake was a kindred spirit in some way, which didn't make sense, as they were so different, but his mom had a soft spot for Blake and would be disappointed it was over. He'd tell her it was okay. He'd reassure her there was someone else in the wings, someone more wonderful, and better suited to him.

It was a lie.

Tommy wasn't interested in dating again, not anytime soon. Being almost thirty, he would of course date again someday, but not soon. Probably not this year. Who knew when he'd be ready? But someday he'd meet the right person, and she'd be beautiful and brilliant, as well as ambitious. She'd have big dreams, but the next time, she'd want his love, and she'd want a future with him. She'd want his children and a life in Montana with him.

He'd find someone who was local, maybe a Marietta girl, and it would be easier. And then maybe, he'd be at peace. Right now he wasn't at peace.

He couldn't even imagine when he'd feel peaceful—or even okay—again.

THE RIDE TO the airport was uncomfortable. Cade and MerriBee drove them, and Cade kept up a conversation with Tommy, discussing horses and cattle and weather and things that allowed them to fill the silence.

MerriBee was quiet, but listening. Blake couldn't focus on any of the discussion. She didn't care enough about horses, cattle, or the weather. She was exhausted, and stressed, and far too emotional. It felt as if they were making a mistake. One of them had to stop this before it was over. Couldn't they work through their differences?

Couldn't they learn to juggle their work responsibilities better?

But finally they were in Cody, and Cade and Tommy pulled the bags from the back of the truck. There were hugs and goodbyes and then Cade and MerriBee were off, and Tommy and Blake entered the terminal, checked in with their respective airlines, before meeting up to go through security together.

It was all quite easy and took little time to reach their gates, which were only five gates from the other. Blake's flight left first, and she'd have a connection in Salt Lake City. Tommy would fly directly into Bozeman and Joe, who was now home, would be picking him up.

They got coffees from the little coffee stand and stood with their drinks, looking out through the glass at the planes arriving and departing.

There was so little to say, and yet she felt everything, and so intensely. Tommy already seemed detached, as if he'd said his goodbye already. Maybe mentally he had. The thought gave her pain. The gate agents arrived at Blake's gate, and people lined up to ask a question or check a seat assignment. It wouldn't be long now, she thought.

"Are we really doing this?" she said, a slight wobble in her voice.

"It's time, don't you think?"

She was grateful he didn't say, *it's what you wanted*, because it wasn't what she wanted now, it didn't feel right now, but her circumstances hadn't changed either. "I will miss you," she said. "I will miss you so much."

"You will be working hard soon, pulling late hours. You'll be busy, and it will help."

"And you? Where do you go from here?"

"Meeting Billy in Texas, and then New Mexico, and possibly after that to Oklahoma. I'm letting Billy choose the schedule. It's really up to him."

"Please be careful."

"Always."

"You're not immortal, you know. You're a man. There are no extra lives."

"I'm aware."

She heard his tone, the flatness in his voice. He truly sounded as if he didn't care, which was worrying. "You have to be safe." She reached out and lightly, gently touched his head. "Wear your helmet."

He caught her hand, pressed a brief kiss to it, before letting it go. "Blake, now it's your turn to make me a promise," he said as the boarding announcement for her flight began. It was a small airport, and they were boarding all rows now. There wasn't much time left.

"I want you to text me when you're home, safe, and then we're going to delete each other's number. We're going to let the other go. I don't think it's smart for us to stay in touch. I don't think it will help either of us move on. We need a clean and total break."

She just looked at him, unable to think of anything to say.

"We should both be notified when the divorce is finalized. In just a few weeks, we'll be single again, and I know you're going to be great when you get home. I know this is what you need. I need a break, too. I need us to be clear that we're not going to try to stay friends. We're not going to be supportive exes. I will always love you, Blake, but it's time we let it all go. Can you do that for me? Just let me go?"

Her heart was thumping. His words filled her with pain. To never speak to him again? To never hear from him again?

Never see him again?

She hadn't seen this coming. Especially not after last night. "Does it have to be so abrupt? Can't we try to be friends?"

"No."

She'd woken this morning praying for a miracle, woken and asked God to find a way. But suddenly she heard MerriBee's words in her head, *He deserves someone wonderful.*

He deserved someone who'd fight for him. Someone who'd give him the support he needed.

Blake knew in her heart that as much as she loved him, she wasn't the best woman for him. She couldn't give him as much as another. She couldn't give him children. She couldn't help create his Wyatt family legacy. Once her cancer reared its ugly head, she'd end up taking more than giving. It was unintentional, but the nature of her health meant she, when ill, sucked everyone dry. She tried to be positive through the treatments, fought to be cheerful, but the bottom line was that her future was uncertain, unpredictable, and for someone like Tommy, possibly unbearable.

And so as they said their goodbyes, she fought to hold her end of the bargain up. She had to stay calm. She had to be unemotional. She needed this to end cleanly. For both of their sakes. Otherwise, this ending would tear them both apart, and she couldn't have that. He didn't deserve that. He needed to move on. Find someone young, strong, healthy… someone perfect for him.

They were making the last call for her flight. There was no more time, just this last goodbye.

She flung herself at him and held him tightly, nose smashed to his chest, inhaling his scent and feeling his warmth and the tough strength that made Tommy Wyatt so special. "I love you," she whispered against his chest, before adding the last bit silently. *I will love you forever.*

# CHAPTER TWELVE

THE SPRING PASSED, the weather warming, the cool morning temperatures giving way to hot summer days.

It hadn't been Tommy's best spring, but then, it hadn't been his worst. He was making the most money when he competed with Billy, so he was focusing on the team events, and not letting the other showings get to him. It wasn't that he was always bad, he was just inconsistent, which wasn't him.

He knew why. His head wasn't in the game. He found it hard to focus. At night when he slept, he inevitably dreamed of Blake. Despite what he'd told her, she was never far from his thoughts. It would be a long time before he wanted anyone else. Not that he wanted her. She'd done a number on his heart, but that was his fault for loving her too much. Wanting her too much.

She was his weakness, and like any weakness, he had to work on it. Work on blocking her out, work on not caring, work on not feeling, work on indifference. Detachment. Apathy.

But it was hard. It wasn't in his nature to hate. So he focused on resolve.

He was not going to let her interfere with his daytime thoughts. He vowed that as soon as she came to mind, he'd have to do something else—going for a run, fifty pushups, working in whatever gym he could find.

He was getting better at forgetting. The sheer physical punishment of running miles and doing hundreds of pushups a day helped.

Tommy and Billy had been traveling together for the past three months, sharing the trailer, and driving time. Tommy had been grateful to have his brother's company. Billy kept him moving, one event at a time, one rodeo at a time.

This weekend, they were in Sisters, Oregon, one of the three biggest rodeos in Oregon each year, with good money for a little town. The Sisters Rodeo had been established back in 1940 and had grown every year until it became a sanctioned PRCA event, which meant, the money was important there, and Tommy and Billy had arrived in Oregon, determined to ride well, rope better, and win.

They arrived Thursday late, set up the trailer, exercised and fed the horses, and got a decent night's sleep. The next morning was more of the same. Tonight's show would start in seven hours. Tommy planned to take a nap if possible. He'd injured his shoulder a couple weeks ago and it still bothered him. Rest was generally the best medicine.

He was asleep when his brother woke him up. "You've

got someone looking for you," Billy said.

Tommy frowned and Billy added, "Not her. Some guy. Said his name was Kendrick. Didn't catch the last name."

*Kendrick?*

Tommy sat up, put his feet on the ground. He'd only ever heard of one person named Kendrick. It wasn't a very common name. "You're sure about that?"

Billy nodded. "Tall, dark hair, kind of nerdy. He's by the first concession stand on the right, just inside the gates."

"I'll be right out," Tommy said, grabbing his boots and putting them on.

"Want me tell him anything?"

"No. I got this."

It had been sprinkling earlier but the sun was shining now, and the sky was almost cloudless, a delicate ethereal blue. Tommy's boots sank into the still damp dirt as he made swift progress from where all the rigs were parked to the stadium entrance.

Inside the gates, he looked for the concession stand. Kendrick was just as Billy described. Tall, lean, with dark hair, dark eyes and black glasses, he looked like someone who'd be in Blake's world.

If this was indeed the same Kendrick.

Tommy approached, not in the best mood. "Heard you were looking for me," he said, by way of greeting.

Kendrick turned, studied him, nodded once. "You really are a cowboy."

Tommy folded his arms over his chest. "What can I do for you?"

"We have someone in common, someone we both care about."

"Not anymore."

"You wait for her for three years and get over her that fast?"

"It's really none of your business, is it?"

"I didn't drive nine hours to play a pissing game. I came to give you some facts she probably should have shared with you, but she didn't."

"Doesn't matter now. We've said our goodbyes. Our divorce was finalized months ago. There's nothing that needs to be said now."

"You're not even curious about the thing she didn't tell you? Probably the most important thing she kept from you?"

Tommy ground his teeth together, furious. "Why are you doing this? Did she put you up to this?"

"She doesn't know I'm here, nor would she want me to be here," Kendrick answered.

"Then get back in your car—"

"She has cancer." Kendrick's voice was hard, unemotional. "Not cancer in remission, but cancer. She was diagnosed in high school, and spent years going through treatments. It got better, and then… it didn't."

Tommy just stared at Kendrick, unable to think of a single thing to say.

"Blake wouldn't want me here telling you this. She'll be angry when she finds out that I tracked you down and told you. But, if you love her a tenth of the amount I think you once loved her, then you should know. Because if I were in your shoes, I would want to know."

Tommy was still struggling to wrap his head around the news.

"Is she dying?" Tommy finally asked.

"Will she die from cancer? Yes. Is she dying this very minute? No. The scans and bloodwork show she's holding her own—" Kendrick broke off, looked away, waited a moment before continuing. "I'm a doctor and I still can't talk about this without getting emotional. Because it's one thing to treat a stranger and another to worry about someone you love. And I do love her. I have always loved her. How can you know her and not love her?"

"So why aren't you together?"

"Because she doesn't love me. She loves you. She doesn't want me. She wants you. And if she's happy, she might actually buy herself more time. But if she's as unhappy as she is now, it's not going to help her. It's not going to keep her around. And I want her around. She deserves to live for as long as she can possibly live."

"But she doesn't want me. She wanted her parents, wanted the city, wanted you."

"Nope. It's not like that, and I don't want to give away too much about her family's situation, but she has spent years undergoing treatment. First in high school, then again in med school—"

"In med school? But I met her in med school."

"She found out mid-January—I think you met in December? Just a month before?—that the malignant cells were active, and growing, and she had to undergo another long round of chemo, really rough chemo, followed by weeks and weeks of radiation. Her insurance didn't want to cover the newest treatment. She wasn't supposed to survive so why should insurance waste all that money? So her parents leveraged everything to make it happen. Her treatment pretty much cleared her family out financially, but the new treatment succeeded. She's still here."

"Thus her interest in medicine," Tommy said under his breath.

"Few people knew what she was going through, especially during med school. I helped her through. I studied with her, quizzed her, even as I made sure she didn't push herself too hard."

"She's grateful. I know she cares about you."

"She loves me, but she's not in love with me."

Tommy was shocked. Devastated. He'd never once considered she might be ill. "Is she sick now?"

"Blake would never want to hear you use the word sick. She doesn't view herself as sick. She views herself as fighting cancer. She views herself as a warrior and she is."

Tommy didn't know what to say. All of his anger, all of

his pain, shifted, fading, deserting him.

Things he hadn't understood before suddenly made sense. Or at least made more sense. Because he'd felt her love. He'd felt her happiness when she was with him. "How is she now?"

"She passed her medical boards. She's working at a family practice group in San Mateo. She's trying to be positive." Kendrick smiled grimly. "But she misses you. She hasn't been the same since she returned from Montana. I hate seeing her this way. Hate seeing her so alone and sad—"

"But you're there."

"Don't be an idiot. I'm not you. She wants you. What's kept her alive is love and hope. Don't take that away from her now."

It was the longest weekend of his life. Tommy couldn't pull out of the events and leave Billy hanging, but it was hard being patient, and waiting for Sunday to come so he could jump on a plane and head to San Francisco. Kendrick had offered to drive him down, but Tommy wasn't interested in spending more time with Kendrick than necessary—and not because there was anything wrong with Kendrick—he was actually a very solid guy, but Tommy had a lot on his mind and a lot to process and he preferred his own company versus nine hours in a car with a virtual stranger.

Sunday, Billy was heading to Boise for the next weekend's competition, and Tommy had promised to meet him there, planning on departing San Francisco Tuesday or Wednesday, depending on how things went with Blake.

That was really the big unknown.

Blake and her secrets.

He was trying to sort through his emotions, because learning about her cancer had changed everything... it explained some things, but created new questions and new frustration.

However, the only person who could answer those questions was her, and so, Sunday, after the presentation of the buckles and money, Billy dropped him off at the Bend airport, and Tommy flew into San Francisco, and got a ride to her apartment building. Kendrick had given him the address and said Blake would probably be home until five or so, when she often joined her parents for Sunday night dinner.

It was almost four when he was dropped off outside her building.

He took off his hat, dragged a hand through his hair, before repositioning the Stetson. He'd come with just a duffel bag and he approached the front door, scanned the names on the outside telecom, and then pushed the button for Eden.

She didn't answer, and he pressed the button again. He wondered if he'd possibly missed her. Had she gone to her parents already?

But just as he was wondering what his next move should be, she said his name, approaching from behind.

She'd been out for a run from the look of it. She was wearing workout gear, had a sweatshirt tied around her waist. Her skin was flushed and damp with perspiration. She'd already removed one ear pod, and was holding the other in her hand, along with her phone and keys. "What are you doing here?" she asked, voice low, cool.

"I was in the neighborhood and thought I'd stop by."

She glanced around at the cluster of apartment buildings, with the 101 Freeway in the background and lifted a brow. "Not really your kind of neighborhood."

"Had a rodeo this weekend so was on the West Coast."

"Where on the West Coast?"

"Bend, Oregon."

"Oh, right around the corner." Her lips curled, but she wasn't smiling. "What *are* you doing here?"

"I wanted to see you."

"We agreed it was over. No contact, no calls. You're not playing by the rules. By *your* rules."

"True."

"So?"

"Things have changed—"

"What's changed?" she interrupted fiercely. "I haven't changed. Have you changed?"

He stared down into her face, holding her hot green-gold gaze. "You were my wife. Don't you think I'd want to know you had cancer?"

❦

IT WAS THE last thing Blake expected him to say. She fell back a step, dumbfounded. How did he know? Who told him?

The only person she'd ever told was MerriBee. "I can't believe she told you." Blake gripped her keys and phone, one key digging into her palm. "She promised me she wouldn't say anything. I trusted her."

"Who are you talking about?" he answered.

"MerriBee. I confided in her when we were in Wyoming, but she swore she'd keep it a secret."

"She did. MerriBee didn't say anything. Kendrick did."

Blake's eyes widened. "You contacted Kendrick?"

"No, sweetheart, he found me. He drove up to Sisters, Oregon, where I was competing this weekend and told me everything."

"He had no right."

"I'm glad he did. I'm glad he loved you enough to tell me the truth. This wasn't something to keep from me. I didn't marry you for just good times. I married you for life. However long that life is. And it kills me that you let me go so easily—"

"Easily?" She choked. "It wasn't easy. I can't sleep. I can't eat. I can barely function. I struggle to get through the day."

"Can we go up to your apartment? Do we have to do this here?"

He was right. This was ridiculously public. She used the

front door key to let them into the lobby, and then pushed the elevator button up. "I can't believe he told you." She looked at Tommy over her shoulder. "He really drove to Oregon to share all the dirty details?"

"They're not dirty details. They're just facts, facts you should have shared with me."

The elevator doors opened. They stepped in and Blake pushed the button for the fifth floor. "Did he show you the statistics? Those are pretty clear."

"He told me there is a lot unknown. You could have two years. He said you could also have twenty—"

"Not twenty. Five if I'm lucky. Probably three. I'm on borrowed time." She faced him in the elevator, arms bundled tightly over her chest. She felt cold. Discussing the end was always scary.

"With new treatments, new medicine, something could change tomorrow," he said. "There are always advances in medicine."

The elevator doors opened. "I know," she said, stepping out. "One of those has kept me here this long."

Tommy followed her down the hall to her door. "There might be another."

"The odds are against it, and you being a numbers guy should know that." She opened her door, stepped in, closing it after he'd entered her apartment.

"I am a numbers guys," he agreed, walking into her living room, his gaze sweeping the small tidy space, with the ivory sofa and the elegant glass and chrome coffee table.

Blake tried to see the apartment through his eyes. Everything was clean and organized. She didn't like clutter, and even to her, her home was on the spartan side. She had a framed black-and-white Ansel Adams photo of Yosemite on the wall. A bookcase filled another wall, books tightly packed. Her white kitchen was spotless, bare except for a single green plant on the edge of the counter. She wasn't a big fan of white spaces, reminding her too much of hospitals, but she wasn't here enough to decorate more, and should she need to move home again, it was better not to have too many possessions.

Tommy's attention returned to her. "I understand statistics, but the data they shared with you is an average. It's averaging those who didn't live long with those who do. And my gut says you're going to live a long, long time—"

"I love your confidence, but you're not a doctor."

He shrugged. "Doctors don't know you. I do."

A shiver raced through her, the hair at her nape rising even as his words buried deep inside of her, filling her heart, and her mind, making it difficult to think or feel of anything but him. The power of him. The power of his faith in her.

The power of his faith, period.

"Explain to me, sweetheart, why you didn't tell me. It's all I've thought of these past three days. It's the question that's running endlessly through my head."

Her eyes searched his and she saw his exhaustion, felt the

pain. His raw emotions shook her. He was always so good at being in control but he was close to breaking now.

"It wasn't to hurt you," she said simply. "It was the one thing I vowed I'd never tell you."

"Why?" he demanded, peeling his coat off and dropping it on the back of the couch. "I *loved* you."

"*Because* you loved me. Because I knew you would move heaven and earth for me. And I couldn't allow it. I couldn't let you, Tommy Wyatt, champion, all-around cowboy, give everything up for me. And when I'm not well, my health becomes exhausting. All-consuming. I'm exhausting and stressful, emotional, frustrating."

"I can handle that."

"And expensive." Her eyes stung with tears she wouldn't shed. "I pretty much destroyed my parents financially. They're going to never have the same security—they've gone through everything—"

"I'm sure they do not have a single regret. You're their daughter, their joy, their everything. It's what parents want to do for their children. It's what you and I would do if we had a child."

"But I can't have children, Tommy."

"Kendrick told me."

She sat down in the gray chair facing the couch. "He said that, too?"

Tommy nodded.

She exhaled slowly. "And yet you want children. It's important to you."

"I did. I do. But I don't want children more than I want you. The dream was to have a family with you. The dream was a life with you. The dream hasn't changed—"

"It hasn't?"

He shook his head. "I still want you. I want every day I can have with you."

She was glad she was sitting. Her insides went hot and cold. Her legs and arms felt shivery and weak. "Still?" she whispered.

He nodded.

Her mouth had gone dry and she was fighting the emotion rising in her. "But, Tommy, I can't be a good wife or a mom. I'm better focusing on a career, giving back through medicine."

"Why do you want to take care of others, but not me?"

"No." She rose, but couldn't move. "That's not how I feel. It's just the opposite. I'm trying to free you so someone better for you can love you—"

"I don't want anyone else. I've only ever wanted you."

"Not when you put me on the plane in Cody."

He crossed to her, wrapped his arms around her, holding her firmly, hip to hip, chest to chest. She'd forgotten his warmth and how solid he was, all muscle and strength.

"Marriage is a partnership, sweetheart," he said, kissing her temple. "I wouldn't just take care of you. You'd take care of me. I mean, I have Billy, but honestly, he's not interested in being my partner. He already has a wife and son. Kind of makes me a third wheel in their marriage."

She chuffed a laugh and pressed her face to his chest, bringing him in. He was everything she loved and needed. Humor. Home.

Safety.

Sanity.

And he'd come for her. He'd come after all. "Please tell me you're not here because you pity me," she said, wrapping her arms around him, holding him tightly, afraid he'd disappear if she let go. "I don't need sympathy—"

"Knock it off. There's no sympathy, just comprehension. There were things I didn't get, pieces missing, but I understand now. You didn't want to be a burden. You're not a burden. You will never be a burden."

She tipped her head up to see his eyes. "The cancer is still relatively dormant, thanks to the hormones I take, but it won't always be. Cancer is smart and aggressive, and it will find a way to break through. It has before—"

"You stopped it."

"Someday we won't be able to." She reached up and wiped a tear trembling on her lashes. She hadn't even realized she'd teared up. "That's not me being dramatic. It's just a fact, and when it comes back, it's going to be rough. My goal was—is—to spare you from that."

Tommy couldn't stand it. He lifted her up, carried her to the couch and sat down with her in his lap. "You don't know me very well, baby, if you think I don't want to be in this fight with you. I've risked everything to win a rodeo event. You don't think I'm man enough to face a tough life with you? You think I'd leave you when you needed me most?"

"I knew you'd say these things. I knew you'd be willing to sacrifice everything for me. But, Tommy, I'm scared. I'm scared of what's ahead. Scared of what I'd put us through."

He didn't say anything.

"Love protects," she whispered. "Love isn't selfish. I wanted to protect you—"

"I'm the one that loves a good fight. Three guys? Bring it on. Four? The party's just getting started." His hand stroked the length of her back and then up again, his touch steady, warm. "If I'm good at anything, it's fighting, hanging tough. I knew from the moment I met you, God had brought us together for a reason. I finally know the reason. I'm here to walk with you through this fire."

Eyes squeezed closed, she pressed her cheek to him, tears slipping out despite her best efforts to hold them back. "I've lived half my life knowing it could end any time. I try to be strong, but sometimes it breaks me. Sometimes I don't know how to accept all the things I'll never have—babies, family." She drew a shuddering breath. "You."

"But you do have me. You've had me from *no, I don't know these guys.*"

She laughed a watery, teary laugh. "Thank God you were there."

"I thank Him, too."

Neither said anything for a long minute. She didn't know what he was thinking, but she was happy just to have him there, holding her.

Sometimes she was fierce, but sometimes she needed someone, and he was her someone. He was the person her heart had been waiting for, looking for. The person who'd be at her side through thick and thin. Someone who cared more about the quality of life, instead of the quantity.

He was the one she wanted, the one she wanted to be with her at the end, whether it was next year, or in ten, or fifty.

*God, it's okay if you give me fifty.*

TOMMY STAYED WITH Blake for the next four days, letting Billy know he'd be flying into Boise Friday morning, well before the rodeo began. While Blake worked, he used her car to take care of business. Monday night, they stayed in, got dinner delivered, and just stayed in each other's arms.

Tuesday night, she took him home to meet her parents. Her dad remembered him, her mom didn't. Initially conversation was stiff but it became more comfortable by the time the evening was over.

Wednesday, he'd made a reservation at one of the nicest restaurants in the city, and over dinner, he proposed, revealing an enormous three carat diamond solitaire. She put it on her finger so fast that he didn't even have to ask what her answer was. They kissed and, instead of drinking the champagne he'd ordered, they left, returning to her apartment to make love.

Thursday night, he and her parents had dinner at a restaurant close to them. They shared their good news—they were getting married soon, and asked for their blessing, hoping they'd be okay with a brief engagement because they didn't want to wait. There was no reason to wait. Life was short, and they loved each other, and there was no time to waste.

Blake's parents were happy for them, truly happy. Her dad even got tears in his eyes, as he hugged Tommy, thanking him for loving his little girl.

Tommy, who didn't tear up easily, felt his own eyes sting and burn. "It's my pleasure," he assured Mr. Eden, giving him another warm clap on the back. "I've loved her for years. I'll never not love her. You can rest easy on that."

Friday morning, Tommy was on a plane to Boise, but as the jet sailed above the San Francisco Bay, he felt as if he was leaving his heart behind. It wasn't forever, though, he reminded himself. He'd be back. Soon. Besides, even though he was gone, he had work to do, and he'd get it done.

Tommy did return soon. Well, relatively soon. He had another rodeo in Deadwood, and then he and Billy drove to the Wyatt ranch where Tommy's truck and rig were waiting. Billy spent a day with the family before continuing to Utah to see his wife and son. Tommy spent another day in Montana with Mom and Granddad, filling them in on everything that had developed, before hitching a different kind of trailer to his truck and starting out early the next morning for California.

It took a day and a half of driving to reach San Mateo, but Tommy was waiting not far from her apartment when Blake returned home from work Friday afternoon. Fridays were her short day, with the office closing at two. He hadn't told her he'd be there, and when she didn't return right away, he wondered if she'd gone to run errands or go see her parents. But just before three, he saw her pull in, and park underground. He called her a minute later.

"What are you doing?" he asked.

"I just got home. What are you doing?"

"Out for a drive."

"That sounds nice."

"Would you like to go for a drive? It's a nice day here."

"Where are you?" she demanded.

"Outside your apartment building."

"I'm on my way."

He'd moved his car while talking to her, so that by the time she stepped out of the apartment building he was right out front, leaning against the 1960 Cadillac.

She froze when she saw him, jaw dropping. "That looks so much like your grandfather's car."

He stepped aside, letting her get a better look. "It is his

car. He's given it to me."

She flew into his arms and hugged him tightly. "What? Why?"

He kissed her once, and then again. "Because he thought it would be a great car for us in California. Certainly better weather than Montana."

"I don't understand," she said.

"I'm moving here. Granddad gave me his car. He's decided we will get more pleasure out of it—"

"Slow down. You're not making any sense. You're moving here?"

"I've bought a house here. It has a big garage, plenty of space for an extra car—"

"You can't move here. You live in Montana."

"People move from state to state all the time. It's actually quite easy to do."

She truly was shocked. "Don't tease me."

"I'm not. I'm quite sincere." He wrapped his arms around her and drew her close, holding her against his chest. "Want to go see our new home?"

She tipped her head back. "*Our* home?"

"If we're getting married—again—we're going to live together this time. Your job is here. I'm moving here. It's settled."

"But your work, the rodeos—"

"Don't worry about those. I go to them. They don't come to me." He kissed her lips, her mouth so soft beneath his. "I probably shouldn't have picked out a house without asking you, but this one came up on the market very fast, and it wasn't going to last, so I made a cash offer, and we should close in a couple weeks."

"Tommy!"

He kissed lower, near the corner of her mouth "Yes, love?"

"What are you talking about?"

"We're going to make this work. We're going to be happy. We're going to have the best life imaginable."

"And Granddad really gave you his Cadillac?"

Tommy burst out laughing. "Is that all you can think about? The Cadillac?"

"It's a very nice car, Tom." But she was smiling, and her eyes were shining. "I love you."

"I know you do." He swung her into his arms and walked to the car, depositing her on the off-white bench seat. "Your parents place is still just twenty-five minutes from our new place. We have a lot of space, so if they want to come live with us, there would be room."

"You've really thought this through," she said.

He went around to the driver's side. "You're all I've thought about since I left for Boise. Well, our life is all I've thought about. Now just try to keep an open mind."

"It's open, but—"

"No buts," he interrupted. "Just have a look first, and then you can tell me your objections."

He started the Cadillac and it came to life with a powerful purr. As he shifted into drive he glanced at her. "What do you think about me going to school?"

She drew her sunglasses from her purse and slipped them on. "Are you thinking about it?"

"Thinking I'll apply in the fall for the following year. I won't know for months if I get in or not—"

"You'll get in somewhere."

"I'm still hoping to compete some," he added, "at least for the time being. And then later, based on which school I'd go to, I can cut back on events, and maybe just do the ones close by."

"You won't make the NFRs that way."

"I've already been a world champion a number of times. I should probably give others a chance."

"That's truly generous of you." She slid across the seat, and used the middle seat belt so that she could sit next to him, hip to hip, thigh to thigh. She rested her hand on his leg, his body so warm through the dark denim. "But Tommy?"

"Yes, sweetheart?"

"I do have concerns. You need land. You need your horses. I can't imagine you trapped in the city."

"Wait until you see where we're going."

"But, Tommy—"

"No buts," he said. "Not yet. Just wait. Hold your judgment until you see what I found for us."

It was an effort, but Blake did as he asked. She didn't protest, even though inwardly she was panicking, but he'd asked her to save her doubts, so she said nothing more, not even after he took the exit for Woodside.

She did shoot him a curious glance then, though.

Woodside was one of the most expensive enclaves in the Bay Area. It was also known as an exclusive town with large lots and luxurious equestrian properties. Had he bought one of those?

They passed palatial homes, and grand estates, mansions hidden behind tall wrought iron fences and ornate iron gates, but continued on to a nondescript road backed by woods.

He turned on the road and they traveled a quarter mile, surrounded by nothing but tall leafy green trees. She glanced up at him and yet his expression revealed nothing.

He drove another quarter of a mile or so, and then got out to open a gate. The gate had a lock on it, and he used a key to remove the lock, and then they drove a little farther until a house came into view.

It wasn't a huge home, but it was a charming shingled two-story house with dark shutters and a circular drive, much like the driveway in front of the Wyatts' log cabin. In fact, there were a lot of similarities to the Wyatt ranch— there were no other homes nearby. Behind the house were sun dappled woods. Off to the side was a paddock, a barn, and another outbuilding.

For a place so close to her work, and the city, it was

amazing.

He glanced at her, pleased with himself. "Well?"

She didn't even want to imagine the cost. "How many acres is this place?"

"Not that many. About five—"

"That's *huge*."

"Even better, the property backs up to six hundred acres of Teague Hill Preserve, permanently conserved land. Which means we have privacy, and space, and I can ride here, and rope and train, and you're still close to work and your family."

She was beginning to feel sick, because if he'd spent all that money... "This would have cost a fortune," she said in a small voice.

"It's an investment. Real estate is a solid investment."

"I thought you were wanting to help Joe on the ranch."

"He doesn't need me now. He might need me one day. We'll see."

"And your mom? And grandfather?"

"We'll still visit them, and they can always come here. We're going to have to get our parents together eventually. I guess at the wedding."

"When is the wedding?" she asked weakly, wondering if he'd planned that already, too.

"I don't know. We'll have to find a date that works for both of us, but hopefully soon, before the summer is over."

This was crazy. Everything was wonderful but crazy. Her

heart was full of so much emotion it made it hard to breathe.

She blinked, clearing her eyes. She had to tell him. She had no idea how he'd react. But they were in so deep now.

"Tommy," she said, quietly, facing him, and taking his hands. "Don't be mad…"

He gave her fingers a light squeeze. "Why would I be mad?"

"You went to all this trouble to buy a place near me, and I know you spent a lot of money for this property. I don't want to even think about how much money you spent."

"Then don't. It was a smart move if it allows me to be close to you."

"But, Tommy, here's the thing." She swallowed hard, and looked up into his gorgeous blue eyes. "I won't be in the Bay Area in another two weeks." She couldn't look away from his gaze, even though she saw the shadows move in. "I bought a business. I'm moving."

"*Where?*"

"Marietta." She touched her tongue to her upper lip, her mouth suddenly so dry. "My parents helped me by cosigning a loan. With their help, I bought Dr. Giddings's practice. I take over August fifteenth."

Tommy just stared at her.

She stood up on tiptoe, kissed his cheek. "Please say something, Tommy. Please."

"But your parents?" he said. "You didn't want to leave them."

"That's the rest of my surprise." She smiled nervously, hoping he'd like the surprise. "They're moving, too. They like the idea of doing something different for the next few years. They're going to lease their house, not sell it, in case they're not happy in Montana, but we agreed we'd all try it together." She smiled faintly. "Along with my uncle. My dad couldn't leave his brother behind, but he's up for it, too. I know it sounds crazy that they've all decided to go with me, but they love me, and want me to be happy, and they know I'm happy when with you." She clasped his hands tightly. "Now please, say something, Tommy."

"It's a little bit weird, me here, and you there, but we could try to make it work."

She laughed and kissed him, and kept kissing him until she felt his hunger and love. "I want to go to Montana," she whispered. "But now we have this place. I had no idea you were going to do this."

"I had no idea you were going to buy Dr. Giddings's practice."

"So what do we do?" she asked, glancing at the charming shingle house with the pretty woods behind it.

"We move to Montana."

"And what about this place?"

"I rent it out to someone, or sell it. I'm not worried."

"You're really okay with us all moving to Marietta?"

"You mean, like one big happy family?" he teased, lifting her off her feet and kissing her.

"Hopefully, we will be." She kissed him back. "My parents are going to lease a house on Bramble. It's an easy walk to Dr. Giddings's practice, so that way I can meet them for lunch some days."

He put her back on the ground and clasped her face. "You've thought of everything."

"I'm type A. Organized and a perfectionist."

He laughed and laughed some more. "I take it you do have some thoughts on the wedding."

She grinned. "Maybe late August? Either in Marietta at the Graff or on the ranch. Whichever you prefer."

"I prefer you," he said.

She wrapped her arms around his neck and pressed close, savoring the feel of him, and the hope she felt for their future. "I know you do. And the feeling is mutual."

# EPILOGUE

*Seven years later*

D R. BLAKE EDEN'S practice in Marietta had grown so much that she'd found another family practice physician to join her. Dr. Marcellus Johnson had grown up in Livingston and had moved away for college but, after ten years of working in Chicago, was looking to move his young family back to Paradise Valley.

Sharing the practice with Dr. Johnson meant Blake could take Fridays off, giving her a three-day weekend with her own family. She and Tommy had been in Marietta for just over a year when they'd heard about three young sisters in need of foster care. The girls had some developmental and behavioral issues and were proving difficult to place.

Tommy and Blake had heard the story on the evening news, and without saying anything to each other, they both independently looked into the requirements for becoming foster parents. Before she spoke to Tommy, she asked her parents if they'd be open to helping them out, should she and Tommy become foster parents. They agreed.

At the end of the week when they sat down to talk,

Tommy and Blake had the same paperwork in front of them. Once again, they had the same idea, and even though Tommy was starting on his degree program, they thought they could make it work.

One month later, Tommy and Blake became a long-term placement for the three little girls who had already been through so much.

Blake took six weeks off from work to help them adjust.

They were afraid of Tommy initially, due to the instability in their home. However, once he introduced them to the animals on the ranch, they began to settle, adapting to their new life with two sets of grandparents and lots of aunts and uncles and cousins who were always coming by the ranch for dinners and holidays and fun.

Two and a half years after they brought the girls home, social services called to let them know the parents of the girls had revoked their rights, and the girls were free to be adopted, should Blake and Tommy be interested in adopting.

They were. It took another few months before the girls were legally their daughters, but once it was all done, they had a big party on the ranch with a bounce house and cake, balloons, pony rides, and homemade huckleberry ice cream made by Granddad.

Blake and Tommy made the decision when they married the second time, that they were going to live fully, joyfully, having adventures, taking risks, being bold, seizing the day. There was much they didn't know, but they made the decision to focus on quality time, not quantity. What mattered was love, and their family, and this incredible, wonderful life they'd built together. Love wasn't just about romance and falling in love. Love was about being best friends and meeting challenges head-on. Love was generous and hopeful and brave.

And because they were brave, Blake was praying for thirty years. *No, make that fifty.*

Why not?

Why not believe?

Why not dream?

Even a little bit of faith goes a long way.

## The End

Don't miss Briar Phillips's story in
MONTANA COWBOY BRIDE!
Coming in April 2023!

Can the magic of the Christmas season lead to a fairy tale happy ending? Find out in ONCE UPON A CHRISTMAS, releasing in October 2022!

# Acknowledgements

The characters in this story had something to say, and I let them tell the story they wanted to tell. Towards the end of the story, I struggled because I believe in happy-ever-afters, but not every happy ending is the same, and not every romance is without heartbreak.

Thank you to my husband who has encouraged me to be myself, and become a hero in my own right.

Thank you to my sons. I love you three.

Thank you to my sister who is always there for big and little things.

Thank you Barbara Ankrum for your editorial expertise—you always know how to save the day.

Thank you to my street team, my readers, my friends, my family.

And thank you to those who lean in when things are hard. You know who you are. I do, too.

xo

# THE WYATT BROTHERS OF MONTANA SERIES

Book 1: *Montana Cowboy Romance*

Book 2: *Montana Cowboy Christmas*

Book 3: *Montana Cowboy Daddy*

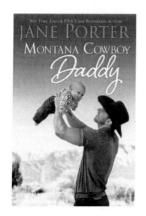

Book 4: *Montana Cowboy Miracle*

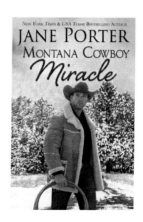

Book 5: *Montana Cowboy Promise*

Book 6: *Montana Cowboy Bride*
Coming in April 2023!

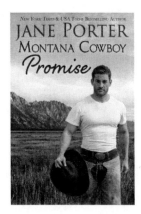

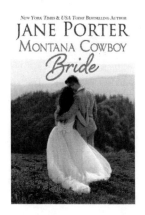

*Available now at your favorite online retailer!*

# More by Jane Porter

*Once Upon a Christmas*
*Coming in October 2022!*


*Oh, Christmas Night*

## Love on Chance Avenue series

Book 1: *Take Me, Cowboy*
Winner of the RITA® Award for Best Romance Novella


Book 2: *Miracle on Chance Avenue*


Book 3: *Take a Chance on Me*


Book 4: *Not Christmas Without You*

## The Taming of the Sheenans series

The Sheenans are six powerful wealthy brothers from Marietta, Montana. They are big, tough, rugged men, and as different as the Montana landscape.

*Christmas at Copper Mountain*
Book 1: Brock Sheenan's story

*The Tycoon's Kiss*
Book 2: Troy Sheenan's story

*The Kidnapped Christmas Bride*
Book 3: Trey Sheenan's story

*The Taming of the Bachelor*
Book 4: Dillion Sheenan's story

*A Christmas Miracle for Daisy*
Book 5: Cormac Sheenan's story

*The Lost Sheenan's Bride*
Book 6: Shane Sheenan's story

*Available now at your favorite online retailer!*

# ABOUT THE AUTHOR

New York Times and USA Today bestselling author of 70 romances and fiction titles, **Jane Porter** has been a finalist for the prestigious RITA award six times and won in 2014 for Best Novella with her story, *Take Me, Cowboy*, from Tule Publishing. Today, Jane has over 13 million copies in print, including her wildly successful, *Flirting With Forty*, which was made into a Lifetime movie starring Heather Locklear, as well as *The Tycoon's Kiss* and *A Christmas Miracle for Daisy*, two Tule books which have been turned into holiday films for the GAC Family network. A mother of three sons, Jane holds an MA in Writing from the University of San Francisco and makes her home in sunny San Clemente, CA with her surfer husband and three dogs.

Thank you for reading

## Montana Cowboy Promise

If you enjoyed this book, you can find more from all our great authors at TulePublishing.com, or from your favorite online retailer.

TULE
PUBLISHING

Made in United States
North Haven, CT
08 April 2022

18001526R00171